SEALS

Tynan moved slowly, his back to the wall. He put his pistol away. Firing it would kill his friends as well as the guard. When he was within striking distance, Tynan's left hand snaked out, snagged the guard, and jerked him to the rear, his hand covering the man's mouth. As the man began to twist and fall, Tynan slammed his knees into the man's spine, dragging him back. He kicked out, trying to escape, but Tynan held tightly. With his right hand on the side of the man's head, Tynan twisted sharply. There was a quiet snap. Tynan felt the man's last breath against the palm of his hand.

Tynan took a deep breath and leaped through the door yelling, "Hit the dirt. Hit the dirt!"

TREASURE!

SEALS #14
TREASURE!

STEVE MACKENZIE

AVON BOOKS ◆ NEW YORK

SEALS #14: TREASURE! is an original publication of Avon Books.
This work has never before appeared in book form. This work is a novel.
Any similarity to actual persons or events is purely coincidental.

AVON BOOKS
A division of
The Hearst Corporation
105 Madison Avenue
New York, New York 10016

Copyright © 1989 by Kevin D. Randle
Published by arrangement with the author
Library of Congress Catalog Card Number: 88-92965
ISBN: 0-380-75772-9

First Avon Books Printing: July 1989

AVON TRADEMARK REG. U.S. PAT. OFF. AND IN OTHER COUNTRIES, MARCA
REGISTRADA, HECHO EN U.S.A.

Printed in the U.S.A.

K–R   10   9   8   7   6   5   4   3   2   1

1

Mark Tynan sat on a recliner, surreptitiously watching the bikini clad girls as they walked around the pool. The suits, he noticed, were getting smaller and smaller, until it looked almost as if they were wearing nothing at all. The bottoms were tiny triangles and the tops narrow bands of colored cloth. Just once he wanted to see one of the girls in the water, or better yet, trying to get out of the water.

"You know," said Stephanie King, "you're not fooling me in the least."

Tynan turned his head so that he could look at her. Sweat from the afternoon sun glistened on her body. As did the oil she'd spread on to keep from burning. She wore a red bikini that contained more cloth than any two of the suits worn by some of the others.

"I'm not trying to fool you," said Tynan, though he was. He wanted to watch the girls without King knowing it, but she was too smart for him, and as an anthropologist, she knew more about human behavior than most people. But she was a good looking woman too. Long hair bleached blonde by the summer sun, bangs that brushed her blue eyes, and a slender body that belied the time spent sitting behind a desk reading long, boring articles about the settlement patterns of the ancient Zuni Indians, or learning more about the sociological ramifications of the introduction of steel axes into the Maloki culture.

"Your eyes are going to fall right out of your head," she said.

Tynan picked up his drink, in a plastic cup rather than a glass and nodded. "I suppose so, but there is no harm in looking."

"None what so ever," said King. "As long as you remember that's all you're doing. Men sometimes forget little things like that."

Tynan swirled the melting ice cube around and then sucked the alcohol from his finger. He could listen to her voice all day long. Low, quiet, gentle and yet sexy. Not the high pitched grating thing that some women used.

"I don't know," said Tynan. "It's like driving down the street and looking at all the other cars. You don't want to trade yours in because it's a good one, but you still want to see the latest models."

"That's a damn sexist thing to say."

Now he grinned. "Oh, and your comment about men forgetting wasn't. This sexist thing works both ways. Some of the women have become female chauvinist pigs."

"Okay," she said laughing. "You win."

"Thank you." Tynan picked up his towel and wiped the sweat from his face. He dropped it back to the concrete and held a hand up, over his eyes to shade them from the afternoon sun. "It's about three o'clock."

"You have somewhere to go?"

"Nope. I'm just getting worried about dinner."

King grabbed a towel and patted the sweat that was beaded near her hairline. She touched her face and then sat up. "You want dinner already, huh?"

"First, anyway," said Tynan.

They stood up, collected their towels, sandals, and Tynan picked up his drink. They walked across the hot concrete, to the grass and then to the front door of the apartment building. King stopped long enough to check the mail and then they walked up to the third floor. She unlocked the door and stepped inside. Tynan followed.

It was a small apartment with a combination dining room and living room, a small kitchen and one large bedroom. But it was cheap, it was clean, and the utilities were covered in the rent so that they could run the air conditioning all the time without going broke.

"Cold," said Tynan.

King threw her stuff on the small dining room table and walked over to the air conditioner, turning it down. She then stretched, as if tired and asked, "You want to use the bathroom first?"

"For a quick shower."

"Go ahead."

Tynan walked down the short hall and turned into the bathroom. It was a very feminine room with a light odor of perfume hanging in the air. The shower curtain was frilly, covered with flowers and the matching rug on the tile floor was beige. He stripped his trunks, turned on the water and held a hand under it until it was warm. He then stepped in, closed the curtain and adjusted the spray.

After a few minutes, he turned off the water and stepped out. Toweling himself, he opened the door and walked over to the bedroom. King sat topless, staring into the mirror over the vanity table. She was studying herself.

Seeing Tynan, she turned. "You look good."

Tynan shrugged. "It's the result of working out all the time."

"That's not what I meant."

Tynan dropped the towel on the floor and then stood there, waiting.

"Guess I'll take a shower now," said King.

"You could have joined me."

"I thought you wanted to go get something to eat," she said.

"I suppose I did."

King left the room and Tynan dressed. He walked out to the living room, turned on the television and crouched in front of it, seeing what was on. There was nothing that caught his interest so he turned it off, and walked to the couch. He sat there and closed his eyes.

For a moment he could see the airport on a Caribbean island. Cuban troops running along a fence, American troops parachuting onto an airfield, and Tynan, along with two others firing on the Cubans. He shook his head and forced the thought out of it. The last thing he wanted to think about was that mission. Or any of his other recent missions.

Instead, he focused on his recent activities, made possible by his leave from the Navy. Thirty days with nothing to do, except chase around the country, if that's what he wanted to do. Rather than that, or visiting his parents, he'd come to visit Stephanie King. When he'd suggested the idea to her, she'd been only too happy to invite him.

King reappeared wearing a light dress. She'd combed her hair until it was glowing. "I'm ready."

Tynan stood. They left the apartment, walked down to the parking lot and got into Tynan's car. It was a rented Ford Mustang convertible that had more than fifty thousand miles on it. Tynan didn't care because he'd wanted a convertible. He liked cruising down the road, the sunlight pouring in on him with the radio blaring.

"Where to?" he asked as soon as they were in the car.

"Anywhere. You pick and surprise me."

He found a quiet restaurant that had once been a factory. The owner had stripped out everything, keeping the shell of the building. Then he'd split it into various restaurants and bars and even added a disco.

They were taken to the second floor where there was a medium priced restaurant. It wasn't that Tynan couldn't afford the more expensive one at the top of the building, but he couldn't see spending the money for atmosphere when he knew that all the restaurants used the same kitchen.

Their table was along one wall with a view out the window. Unfortunately, the only thing to see out the window was the parking lot of the shopping center across the road. A four tier shopping center that looked as if it had been designed for function rather than esthetics.

The cocktail waitress in an abbreviated costume that showed her legs and most of her breasts took a drink order and another waitress, in a more sedate costume, took their food order.

With that done, King leaned forward, reached across the table and said, "We have to talk."

"Oh oh," said Tynan.

King laughed. "No, it's nothing like that. It's a very simple thing, really."

The cocktail waitress brought the drinks, set them in front of them and disappeared. Tynan picked up his bourbon, took a sip and then said, "Go ahead. Do your worst."

King rocked back. She picked up her Bloody Mary, took out the celery and put it on the table. After sipping it, she said, "I've got an assignment."

"When do you have to leave?" Tynan asked immediately, thinking of three weeks of leave he had remaining with nothing interesting to do.

"A couple of days." She laughed. A single, short laugh. "It's your fault, actually."

"Great. I'm to blame."

"Indirectly." She glanced out the window and then back at Tynan. She lowered her voice. "It's almost a direct result of our ah, adventure, in the south. In Honduras."

"How so?"

King picked up her napkin and played with a frayed corner of it, pulling at the loose threads. "Gave the powers that be the itch for more treasure. When we found that old Mayan city filled with the relics of the past, not to mention the gold and silver, they learned how simple it was to find gold. And we had it in our hands when we were there. Well, not in our hands exactly, but we had the opportunity for millions of dollars in gold, silver and emeralds. The value of them, just in the grossest sense, in terms of money only, was what? Two hundred million? Five hundred million?"

"Maybe more."

"And as artifacts, statuettes, jewelry and the like would double, triple the value. And that's without even considering the academic benefits."

"Triple it, at the least," agreed Tynan.

"Now, for a few thousand dollars invested, they could have all that gold in their hands. Not now, but earlier, they could have. Enough money for the university to run into the far distant future."

Tynan finished his bourbon. "I thought you academic types were above all that. Money isn't important. It was the opportunity to learn."

"You believe that and I'll show you a second rate school with no football team."

"Oh. There a point to all this?"

They've been bitten by the gold bug." She grinned.

"You know, a university, with the resources that it controls, is the perfect place to launch a treasure hunting venture."

"You've got to be kidding."

"Think about it. Researchers who love to pour over old manuscripts. Experts in language. Experts in ancient civilizations and the exploration of the New World. Scientists from every discipline who are on staff and who can be used as the need arises."

"Granted," said Tynan. He stopped as the waitress brought the salads. When she left them again, he added, "but universities are above those things."

"No, the grab for glory usually takes a more esoteric approach, but on Saturday you'll find the most conservative professor in the stands cheering for the team. And now they've seen the light."

"Okay," said Tynan. "I believe you."

"So, for the last several months, they've been researching every old treasure story they could find, figuring on exploiting those that seemed to be based in fact."

Tynan put down his fork and said, "I thought the government had some kind of claim on all treasures found in the United States."

"The point is debatable and is being contested in court, but the general rule seems to be finders keepers. And once again the university environment proves my point. Some of the finest lawyers in the country teach here. They're well versed on the various aspects of the law."

Tynan burst out laughing. "I can see the eminent lawyer arguing the premise of finders keepers."

"It's not that simplistic, but you get the point."

"So, you're going after a treasure."

King shrugged. "There are some well established treasures waiting to be found."

"Such as?" said Tynan.

The waitress was back with the main course. When she had set the plates down, Tynan held up his glass. "Hit me again."

"Certainly. And you?" she asked, looking at King.

"I'm fine." When the waitress was gone, King said, "How about the Oak Island treasure?"

"Never heard of it," said Tynan, cutting into his prime rib.

"It was first discovered in 1795. Or rather, I should say the location was discovered then by three teenagers on Oak Island just off the coast of Nova Scotia. They dug down to thirty feet, tearing through wooden platforms every ten feet. When they reached the third of the platforms they realized they needed some help. They interested some of the locals in the idea and the search continued off and on. Has continued on and off until today."

"But no treasure," said Tynan.

"Well, after several weeks, they got down to a hundred, hundred ten feet and left the pit for the night. Didn't get down there in one day, you understand, but finally managed it. When they returned, the following morning, the pit was filled with water."

"Rain?"

"No, it wasn't fresh." She ate for a moment and then continued. "Someone finally noticed that the water level in the pit changed with the tides which meant it was connected with the nearby ocean. At the closest beach they found that someone had created an artificial beach that was a large filtering system that allowed the water to drain along a conduit system and fill the pit."

Tynan was suddenly impressed. "Seems like quite an engineering feat."

"It was. The treasure hunters blocked it off and tried to pump out the pit. Didn't work. Over the next two centuries, they've tried repeated things to get down to where they believe the treasure is buried."

"They sure one's down there?"

King shrugged. "No one believes that someone would go to all that trouble to build such an elaborately booby-trapped pit without putting something of great value down there. It was designed well enough to even stop the finest engineering minds of our time."

"Okay," said Tynan. "One treasure that no one has been able to get to."

King took a bite of her dinner, chewed and then swallowed. "That's only one. The various archives in Spain are filled with the accounts of treasure ships that were lost on their way from the New World to the Old. Millions of dollars, billions, on the sands in the shallows between Florida and Cuba. Well documented treasures."

"Which no one can get to."

King grinned. "Well, someone with training in SCUBA might be able to locate something down there. You can get to them. You just have to know where to look."

"That where this is going?" asked Tynan. "You want me to go along as an advisor because of my Naval training?"

"No," said King. "The problems in that are numerous and don't seem to be worth the effort. At least for our purposes right now."

"Unless you find something," said Tynan.

"There are easier places to search."

Tynan finished his dinner and pushed the plate aside. "Where?"

"The desert Southwest," she said. "There are hundreds of tales. The Lost Adams, the Lost Dutchman, and the lost treasure of the Zunis."

"I've heard of that Lost Adams," said Tynan.

"It was the basis for the movie, *Mackenna's Gold*.

They did a pretty good job of telling the legend. The problem is that it's a mine and not a treasure. You'd have to dig the stuff out and refine it. Besides, there's a tale in archaeological circles that a white man found it again in 1928."

"What?"

King smiled. "An archaeologist who was interested in cliff dwellings was shown the one near the Canyon of Gold. You remember in the movie there was a big fist fight near it. At the foot of the cliff dwelling. Anyway, an Indian guide took this archaeologist into the canyon to show him the cliff dwelling and told him to look down, near his foot. There was a huge gold nugget next to his boot. The guide told him if he touched it they both would be dead in a matter of seconds. After they both got out of there."

"But at the end of the movie, the canyon disappeared in a cloud of dust from an earthquake."

"Yes," said King. "That comes from a man named Baxter. He claimed that he found the Canyon of Gold. He and a friend got out of it and tried to return later, claiming that the way was blocked by a rock slide caused by an earthquake. But that was before the archaeologist got in. We suspect that everything is still there, if you know where to look."

"So that one's out too."

"Certainly. As is the Lost Dutchman. Again, it's a mine and not a treasure and quite a few people have been killed looking for it. Every year a couple of people die in the search. The terrain is too rugged and there are rumors that someone has found it and is killing anyone who gets too close to the hidden entrance."

"All right," said Tynan. "You're not going after either of those because they would require additional work to exploit them. Just where in the hell are you going?"

"You won't tell, will you?"

"Who would I tell?" He finished his drink and set the glass on the table. Hell, if you'd like, I'll go with you. For three weeks, anyway."

"Yeah, I'd like that."

"So where are you going?"

"Fort Huachuca, Arizona."

2

The desert stretched out in front of him like a lumpy blanket spread out for a picnic. The bush and cactus were scattered randomly over the dry sand. In the distance, shimmering in the heat of the late afternoon sun were the mountains. Far to the south, across the border was Mexico. To the north, out of sight was Tucson, and to the east, also out of sight, was Tombstone, the scene of the famous gunfight and the most famous of the boothills.

Lloyd Jefferies, leaning on the sun-hot hood of his old Willie's jeep, watched as two people walked in the desert far below him. Both wore backpacks, hats, shortsleeve khaki shirts and khaki shorts with khaki knee socks. They seemed to have a destination somewhere to the north of where they were. Jefferies didn't like that. He didn't like anyone walking the desert near him, especially that particular section of the desert.

He straightened up and walked around to the passenger's side of the jeep. Carefully, he stored the binoculars in their leather case and set them in the rear, next to the ice chest that contained a supply of Milky Way candy bars, half a gallon of fruit juice and a dozen apples. He then picked up the rifle case, which was near the two five gallon cans of water, and sorted through a ruck sack that contained survival rations, clean socks, a hunting knife, flashlight and matches, taking out a fifty-round box of ammo.

Unzipping the rifle case, he pulled from it the Winchester Model 79, a civilian version of the modified weapon used by Marine Corps snipers in Vietnam. He loaded it carefully, worked the bolt to chamber a round, and then returned to the front of the jeep.

In the distance, he could barely see the two figures walking. Blurs created by their motion, their distance, and the sun baking the sand, the heat radiating up from it. For a moment he watched the two people, but their path didn't vary. They seemed to be walking straight for the hidden entrance a mile or so from them.

Jefferies pushed his hat back on his head and leaned across the hood of the jeep. The sun had heated it so that the metal was almost too hot to touch. Carefully setting the rifle near the windshield, he returned to the rear of the jeep and extracted a blanket. Folding it, he laid it on the jeep and then leaned across it. Wrapping the sling of his rifle around his upper arm to steady it, he aimed at the two figures walking across the sand.

The ART scope brought them into sharp focus again. Not as clearly as the binoculars, but close enough. He tracked them for a moment, then, leading one of them by almost four feet, he slowly squeezed the trigger. The weapon fired abruptly, slamming back into his shoulder. The bang seemed to echo through the hills around him, but neither of the figures heard it or looked toward him.

He worked the bolt rapidly, extracting the spent cartridge which bounced off the windshield, and aimed at the second figure. But he didn't fire immediately. He waited to see if the first shot was good.

One of the figures stopped suddenly and then fell to the side. The other stood there, facing Jefferies, but looking down at his fellow, not understanding what had happened. Then it crouched, as if to give aid. As it did, Jefferies fired again, at the now nearly motionless target.

He worked the bolt, but kept his eye on the figure with the crosshairs off to the left side. A light, steady breeze was blowing and Jefferies figured it would push the slug toward the center of his victim.

The round hit a moment later. Jefferies could see nothing, other than the reaction. The force of impact knocked the person back, off balance. He waved his arms for an instant as if to keep from falling and then toppled over.

Jefferies used the scope to watch both victims, but neither of them moved again. They lay where they had fallen. Satisfied that they weren't faking, he plucked the blanket from the hood and walked around to the driver's side of his jeep. He tossed the blanket into the rear and then carefully set his rifle in it. Finally he climbed behind the wheel and started the jeep's engine.

Slowly he drove down to where the bodies of the two people were lying. At first, he couldn't see the bodies because of the lay of the land, but he came up suddenly, out of an arroyo, to a slight rise and could look down on them. Two people sprawled on the ground, both on their backs, their packs giving them an unnatural, uncomfortable look.

He stopped less than five feet from the bodies. He took his .45 automatic and stuck it in the waistband of his khaki trousers. Then he climbed out of the jeep and walked over to the bodies. The second victim was dead, the bullet having shattered the breastbone, exploding shards of bone through the body to rupture the heart and fray the lungs. The front of his shirt was soaked blood red and there was a pool forming under him. His eyes were open, staring up at the unforgiving sun.

He turned to the second body, the first he'd shot. Now that he was close, he could see that it was a girl. He'd suspected that, but the distance, the bulky back pack, the hat and loose fitting clothes had made it difficult to tell. Not that it would have made a difference even if he'd been sure before he pulled the trigger.

He crouched near her and as he did, she opened her eyes. For an instant she was staring into the pale blue sky, unaware that anyone was near her. Then she saw him. She stared straight at him. "Help," she said, her voice low, almost impossible to hear even in the quiet of the desert.

She was a pretty girl. Long blonde hair that had spilled out when she lost her hat. Her face was a pasty white, waxy looking. The wound was in her shoulder, high enough to have missed everything vital. He imagined that she'd have trouble using her arm, if she survived. Blood stained her shirt, soaking the side nearly to the waist.

Grinning, Jefferies said, "Take it easy. I'm here now."

It looked as if she tried to smile back at him, but failed. Too much pain from the shoulder wound.

Jefferies unbuttoned the top of her shirt and pulled it open, as if to inspect the wound. Carefully, he folded the material out of the way, but he wasn't interested in the wound. He wanted to see her breasts, and she didn't resist, believing he was there to help her.

"Easy," he said as he pulled the material out of the way. He studied her chest for a moment, thinking that it was a shame. She was a very pretty girl. She had a good looking body, now that he was close enough to study it.

He pulled his handkerchief from his hip pocket, shook it out, and pressed it against the wound in her shoulder. As he did, he managed to squeeze her breast, but she seemed not to notice the pressure of his fingers.

"What were you doing out here?" he asked.

Her eyes fluttered and opened again. She looked up at him and tried to form words. The lips moved slightly but there was no sound.

"You shouldn't have been out here," said Jefferies. "Not alone and unarmed."

"Hiking," she said. "Hiking."

"That all?"

"Water."

"In a moment." Gently he laid her back and then stood up. He studied her carefully, wishing that he hadn't shot her. He'd have preferred capturing her and taking her back to the line shack he sometimes used. There he could have used her to cook and clean and service him whenever the need arose. Wounded, she was worthless to him, even though she had a good body. Slender, with long legs. Pretty. It was too bad.

She glanced up at him and reached toward him with one hand. "Water."

Jefferies shrugged and took out his pistol. He aimed at her face and pulled the trigger once. She spasmed in death. Her legs kicked out and she rolled to her side. Blood and brain stained the sand around her.

"Too bad," he said out loud.

Bending down, he went through her pack and that of her companion. There was nothing to indicate they were searching for anything. Out on a survival hike, or a nature walk, but nothing more. Too bad they had blundered into that section of the desert. But those were the breaks.

He stripped the packs from the bodies and then went through the pockets, stealing the wallets. He stole their watches and rings and then, thinking about it, used his knife to cut the clothes from both of them. If someone came across the bodies before the buzzards and coyotes and gila monsters got to them, there wouldn't be much in the way of evidence to identify the bodies.

As he stood up to return to his jeep, he suddenly realized they would have to have driven out into the desert, but he'd seen no sign of a vehicle. He turned slowly, scanning the desert but saw nothing. He got his binoculars out and again searched but their car or truck was nowhere around.

He'd have to find it. But before he left, he took a Polaroid camera from the rear of the jeep. He stood over the girl and took a picture of her head and shoulders, showing both the wounds. He moved to the boy and did the same, turning it so that he could get the face in the shot. He hadn't been a bad looking kid either. Light brown hair cut fairly short. A deep tan. Well muscled. It was too damn bad.

He climbed into his jeep having taken the pictures. He set the camera in the back, and then started the engine. He turned and followed the path that the hikers had used, their footprints easy to follow in the desert. After more than a mile, he found their car, an old Ford. It was parked on the side of a dirt road, concealed behind a large bush.

Jefferies took the backpacks from his jeep and carried them to the Ford. He searched the boy's and found the car keys in it. He unlocked the door, threw the packs into the back and then climbed behind the wheel. He drove the car up on the road, pulled it to the side and then got out, leaving the keys in the ignition. The way things were that close to the Mexican border, the car would be gone before nightfall, the evidence disappearing into Mexico before the police even knew that the kids were missing.

Walking back to his own jeep, Jefferies felt better. The evidence would be gone in hours, the bodies would probably never be found, and his secret was safe. No one would get to the treasure before he did, and that was all that mattered.

Army Captain Jason Collins sat behind his massive desk and read the letter again. It wasn't much of a surprise since he received two or three of them a week. Requests from civilians who had heard that two hundred million dollars in Spanish gold and silver was hidden somewhere on the Fort Huachuca grounds. Rumors of the wealth had persisted, even when Collins had issued news releases claiming that a complete survey of the Huachuca military reservation had been made by the Army. He explained that no gold had been found. No hidden tunnels had been found. And no one had listened to him.

The public assumed, because nothing had been found, that it was still there. They rejected the idea that the Army would line up its troops, shoulder to shoulder, and send them across the open grounds, looking for an unknown opening. If there was a hidden tunnel anywhere on the military reservation, it would have been found.

Now another group was asking permission to search for the treasure on Fort Huachuca. Collins had his instructions. The answer was no, only because the post commander didn't want dozens of civilians on the fort tearing up the grounds in search of a treasure that he didn't believe existed.

Collins sat for a moment in his small office. It contained his desk, a couple of chairs for visitors and a small bookcase holding binders with the regulations that governed the operation of his office.

Collins himself was a young man, only twenty-six. His commission was the result of ROTC, taken on a college campus when the majority of the students were threatening to burn the ROTC building to the ground and to stone all

those who were members of the ROTC. But there were
scholarships to be had, for those who didn't mind being
shouted at once in a while. And there was the promise of a
job on graduation. With the Vietnam War in full swing,
promotions were fast, which explained his rapid rise to
captain.

Collins stood up and moved to the outer office where
Sergeant Sheila Davis was typing rapidly. She was a
young, pretty woman, with black hair and a slender body.
She had a scar on her face, the result of a run-in with her
brother when she was eleven. She thought it destroyed her
looks, but it was now almost impossible to see.

Collins tossed the letter into her "in" basket. "Standard
negative reply for the treasure hungers."

She stopped typing and looked up at him. "Yes sir." She
turned back to her typing, stopped again and looked up at
Collins again. "You're sure there's nothing to this?"

Collins shook his head. "Sheila, don't let them fool
you. If there was anything hidden out there, we'd have
found it a long time ago."

"I was talking to some sergeants at the club last night
and they were talking about heading out, to the south
where the country gets rough. They said no one had ever
really looked out there."

Collins rubbed his face. "Don't you start on me."

"Well, why couldn't there be some treasure buried
somewhere out there?"

"Sheila, have you ever read one account of anyone,
anywhere ever finding a huge treasure? There are stories of
lost wealth from all over the world, from King Solomon's
Mines to the Lost Adams which is just across the border in
New Mexico, and I've never seen one shred of evidence
suggesting that any of these treasures or lost mines exist."

"Still . . ."

"So you've caught it now."

She stared at him, a puzzled look on her face. "Now I've caught what?"

"The treasure bug. We all get it when we get here. We hear the stories of untold wealth hidden by the Spanish before they were wiped out by the Apaches, or hidden here by the Aztecs to keep it away from the Spanish. A cave filled with gold bars. We begin to wonder if there isn't something to the story. And what we'd do with all that gold."

"And?" she asked.

"We spend our free time driving the back roads and hiking in the desert looking for the cave. I even pulled all the old maps of the post I could find, hoping to uncover a clue that no one else had found. But that all came to nothing. The treasure just doesn't exist."

She turned to face him, sliding her chair around, away from her typewriter. "How do you know?"

"Because it's like the pot of gold at the end of the rainbow. The trick is, there is no end to the rainbow. There is no treasure here."

"I think there is," she said. "Just because you didn't find it, doesn't mean it's not out there. Where there's smoke, there's fire."

"Fine," said Collins, nodding. "When was the last time you heard of anyone finding any treasure?"

"Wasn't there a guy up in Colorado who found a sack of gold coins?"

"Sure. Thirty thousand dollars probably lifted from a stagecoach. But that's not two hundred million in gold buried by the Spanish."

"You've become cynical," she said.

"No, just realistic." He sat on the edge of her desk and tried not to look at her legs. "With all the rumors of gold around here, if it had existed, someone would have found it by now. I mean, we're talking about two hundred million dollars in a fairly well defined geographical location. Everyone around here's heard of it but no one has found it."

"Maybe it's just hidden better than you thought."

"Maybe it just doesn't exist." Collins stood up. "Anyway, send those people the standard negative reply."

"Yes sir." She hesitated and then asked, hastily, "Will you help me search for the treasure?"

Collins laughed. He turned and looked at her and started to say no, but then suddenly, changed his mind. "On one condition. You pack the lunch."

"Deal."

"Saturday morning," said Collins, "but you can't tell anyone the real reason we're going out there."

"Afraid they're going to beat us to the treasure?"

"No," said Collins seriously. "I'm afraid they're going to laugh at us."

3

The next morning, King and Tynan drove out to the university. In the heat of the summer, the number of students had been reduced. The majority of them were gone, home for vacations or working summer jobs so that they wouldn't have to work during the school year. The number of students had been reduced to a third of what it normally was. Classes were more informal and held daily.

Many of the regular professors and graduate students were off trying to improve their knowledge of the world. They were studying the things they didn't get the chance to study during the academic year. In a few cases it meant that they were studying each other in exotic locales, but for the most part, they were conducting serious research that would be analyzed at length during the rest of the academic year.

The major exception seemed to be the Department of Anthropology and Antiquities. Everyone, both professors and graduate students, was there, waiting. Secretaries were on the phones arranging travel, lining up hotel rooms, and organizing the small details of a major expedition.

Tynan had to laugh when he saw all the activity because

he knew the destination of the expedition. Arizona. Not exactly the desolate back water that some would have everyone believe. Savage Indians did not roam the land. There were no dangerous beasts, other than a few rattlesnakes which the clever person could avoid, or the gila monster that anyone could outrun.

And they'd be living in the Holiday Inn or a Best Western, driving out to the search areas during the day. Maybe they'd stay in the field overnight. Maybe not.

King dragged him through the outer offices that showed their age. Not the modern glass and steel cubes but something that had been constructed during the Victorian Era when ceilings were twelve feet high and the wooden appointments were ornately carved. Now they looked strangely old fashioned, making Tynan think he'd stepped back in time, to a world that no longer existed. One where academic achievement was more important than financial wealth.

They walked into a conference room that was constructed along the same lines as the offices. A high ceiling with huge lights that cast pools of brightness. Tall windows that looked out on a heavily wooded campus. Sidewalks filled with students walking to a class or heading home. If it hadn't been for the modern cars on the streets, and the shorts and T-shirts of the men and women, Tynan could almost believe that he had moved back in time.

"Be seated," said one of the men.

Tynan took a place at the table. A heavy, wooden thing with carving around the edges. The shine had dulled during the decades it had stood there. Opposite the window were wooden bookcases filled with leatherbound volumes.

"Doctor King," said the man, "I don't approve of your unilateral invitation to an outsider."

"Doctor Chapman, Mister Tynan has assisted us in the

past and his help may prove invaluable on anything that we plan for the future."

"I'm not contesting that," said Chapman. "I'm saying that I do not approve of your unilateral action."

"If there is a problem," said Tynan, "I can leave."

"No, Mark, you sit down," said King. "I want you here and since I'm going to be the advance party, all the advance party, what I say goes."

"We could rethink that," said Chapman.

"Stop being an ass," said King. "He's here and he knows. I'm here and I know. Cutting us out now isn't the answer. Use the talents we have and stop trying to be a little Hitler."

For a moment Chapman sat quietly, as if considering the question. Suddenly he nodded and said, "Makes sense. Especially if he knows already."

"Then let's get on with it."

Chapman nodded again and moved to the door, closing it. He looked at the assembled group. King and Tynan had been the last to arrive. Hopkins, Luis, and McGee had already been there and none of them had much to say. There was an easel in one corner that was covered.

Chapman sat down at the head of the table and said, "Luis, what have you learned?"

Luis opened a folder in front of her. She was a small woman with dark hair, delicate features and a Latin cast to her skin. "The records, as best as we can piece together in Mexico City and in Seville, suggest that the treasure in the Fort Huachuca area is the result of a plundering first of the outposts of the Aztec Empire, and then mining operations conducted in northern Mexico and the southern areas of the United States."

"Then there is a historical precedence for this?' said Chapman.

"Certainly. We know of a dozen different locations where mining operations produced silver or gold. We know of instances where circumstances prevented the various Spanish officials and soldiers from delivering the gold to the sea for shipping to Spain. The question is not whether the various treasure troves exist, but where they happen to be hidden and how easy it will be to get to them."

King leaned close to Tynan. "Convinced?"

"I'm becoming a believer," he whispered to her. "But very slowly."

"Now," said Luis, "we've isolated several of these, and as I said last week, the best bet is the Huachuca horde." She stood and moved to the map. As she pulled the cover to the side, she added, "Here, on the eastern side of the military reservation is where we need to concentrate."

"Maps available?" asked Chapman.

"Yes."

Chapman looked at King. "You should be there sometime in the next two days for the preliminary work which shouldn't take more than a week."

"I don't have a problem with that," she said.

Chapman waved at the rest of the people at the table. "Are there any other questions?"

Now Tynan spoke. "I know that people have been murdered searching for the Lost Dutchman, and Stevie here told me of Apaches who apparently still guard the Lost Adams. There anything like that here?"

"Nothing that we know of. The Superstition Mountains are isolated and rugged. It would be possible, it is easy, for people to disappear in there. At Huachuca, it is open and accessible. No recent disappearances or murders have been reported in the vicinity."

Chapman glanced at Tynan and then the others. "Maybe I should make one thing clear here. This treasure is not something that only we know of. Granted with the work of Doctor Luis, we've been able to document its existence and do a better job of pinpointing the location of it, but we are not the only ones who know about it. We must maintain secrecy, only to protect the reputation of the university, not because there would suddenly be bands of treasure seekers fighting us. I anticipate no danger to anyone on our party, even if we announce, upon arrival, our reasons for being there."

"Well," said Tynan looking at King. "It should be fun, anyway."

When the meeting broke up, they left the university and drove to King's apartment. There, with a beer in hand, Tynan looked over all the material they had been given for the day. He spread the maps out and then laughed.

"What's so funny?" asked King from the bedroom where she was changing clothes.

"One of these great maps, obtained at who knows what risk, is nothing more than a road map like they hand out in filling stations."

"So, what's your point?"

"We're mounting this great expedition and we're using maps from the Texaco Station?"

She came out of the bed room wearing shorts and a light blouse with the tails hanging down. She pulled out a chair close to him and dropped into it. "Again. So what?"

Tynan shrugged. "So nothing."

She shifted the papers around and studied the map of the Fort Huachuca area. "Seems to me," she said, "we'd be in the best shape if we stayed in Sierra Vista. Fairly large town and no one would notice a couple of strangers."

"With a military post nearby, no one's going to pay

much attentions to strangers," said Tynan. "New people would be sent to the fort all the time."

"So, we fly out tomorrow. Into where? Tucson? And then rent a car?"

Tynan looked at the map. "Probably be easy to fly into Tucson. Looks to be no more than an hour or so from Tucson into Fort Huachuca. Then we scout around, find what we need and call in the rest of your team."

"Or we could drive out," said Tynan. "No reason to fly. It's, what, a thousand miles? That would put us into the area with a car and would save the university money for airline tickets."

"Save you money on them too," said King.

"I can always fly free on a military plane. Catch one into Davis-Monthan. Look at all the old aircraft stored in the desert. Row upon row of airplanes. So it doesn't bother me. I just think we'd be better off driving in."

"Great," she said, slapping the map. "Now that we've gotten that settled, what do we do until tomorrow?"

"Wait. Are we driving or flying?"

"You want to drive. We drive. Now, again, what do we do until tomorrow?"

"Eat dinner?" suggested Tynan innocently.

"Jeez, I was told to watch out for sailors because they're all such coxmen. And what happens. I find the only man in the Navy who likes to eat."

"You know, talking like that could get you into real trouble real fast."

"I hope so."

Jefferies drove back along the track that he had made when he left the bodies. As he approached them, he could see buzzards circling overhead. But even though he knew what to look for and where to look, he didn't see the bodies until he was close to them.

He stopped the jeep and walked around the front of it then, studying the sandy ground, looking for anything he might have left. Clues. He wanted to make sure that the local police and sheriffs, if they got out there, wouldn't have any clues. Satisfied that he'd left nothing, he walked over to the woman and stared down at her body.

That had been a real shame. She was so pretty. Or rather had been so pretty. And he didn't like killing women. They were useful in so many other ways. But she was no longer pretty and already her body was beginning to dry up under the brutal Arizona sun.

Jefferies scanned the horizon all around, but there was no one to be seen. High overhead was a jet, the four engines under the wings creating a vapor trail, but it was so high that no one in it could see him and the dead bodies.

He climbed into the jeep and drove off, this time toward the east and the highway there. He came up over a rise and slowed down. When he saw there was no traffic on the road, he drove down to it and then turned to the south and Bisbee. Time to get home so that the wife didn't worry about him. Time to get home so his partners didn't worry.

Along the way, he turned down a dirt road and stopped out of sight of Highway Eighty. He got out, took the clothes he stripped from the hikers and piled them in a ditch. Then, using some gas from the five gallon cans that he carried, he soaked the clothes. Standing back, he tossed a match into the pile and watched as they burned. He used a stick picked up near him to stir the fire, making sure that they were well burned. When the flames died, he kicked the ashes apart and then pushed sand over them, hiding them. The last bit of evidence was gone.

Jefferies then got back into the jeep and drove to Highway Eighty and turned southeast toward Bisbee. He saw a number of cars outside a roadhouse that promised beer, cold drinks, and cocktails. Recognizing two of the cars, Jefferies pulled in, parked and climbed out.

Before he reached the door, he heard the music blaring. Country music from amplified speakers seemed to vibrate the walls. Jefferies grabbed the wooden handle of the door and swung it open. Cool air boiled out at him and under the music, he heard the babble of voices.

Once inside, he saw a group of men around a pool table, a lamp hanging down over it. There was a bar in the back and each of the seven stools was occupied. Along one wall was a row of booths and there were four or five tables near them. Two couples tried to dance on the miniature floor. Pinball machines took up space on the other wall.

Jefferies saw two of his partners sitting in the rear booth, each with a beer in front of him. He moved to the table, saw the young, tired waitress glance at him and yelled, "Bring me a Coors."

He slipped into the booth with them and leaned forward, elbows on the table. "You can thank me now."

The bigger of the two, Nate Winters, rubbed a hand through his thick, greased down hair. He was a rotund man, once stocky and strong, and a football player in high school, but now mostly fat. He had small eyes, a large mouth and broken nose. He wore a dirty T-shirt and blue jeans.

"Thank you for what?"

The waitress appeared with the beer. She put the bottle on the table and then retreated.

Jefferies picked up the bottle by the neck, tilted it to his mouth and drank. Then holding it there, he whispered, "I caught two people walking in an area where they shouldn't be walking." He raised his eyebrows.

"And?" prompted John Boyle. He was a slight man, thin almost to the point of looking sick. He had longish brown hair that the others told him made him look like a hippie. He had sunburned skin that never seemed to tan, though he'd lived in Arizona all his life. His features were fine, his eyes blue and his hands were very small.

Again Jefferies tilted the bottle to his mouth, his elbows on the table, so that he could drink. "And, the problem has been eliminated."

"Eliminated how?" asked Winters.

"Permanently," said Jefferies.

"Just what happened out there?" asked Winters as he looked around to make sure that no one was listening to them.

"Saw some people walking toward the cave mouth. Walking right toward it. I stopped them. With my rifle."

"You hide the bodies?"

"Stripped them and left them," said Jefferies. "Too bad too. The girl was a looker. Didn't know it though because I was too far off when I saw them."

"You just left the bodies?"

"Coyotes'll get them," said Jefferies.

"Shit," said Winters. "That was fucking stupid."

"They were walking right at the cave mouth," said Jefferies. "It was the only thing I could think of to keep them away from it."

"Not that," snapped Winters. "Leaving the bodies. They get found and there's going to be police and sheriff's deputies, and searchers all over the damned place. Someone might stumble into the wrong hole."

Jefferies shrugged. "So we go out and move them. No big thing."

"I wished you'd a thought a that before you come here," said Boyle.

"No one's ever out there anyway," said Jefferies. "Figured it was no big thing."

"Tomorrow we go move them," said Winters.

"Tomorrow's Saturday,' said Boyle.

"So what?" asked Winters. "With what we got out there, a little inconvenience won't hurt. Won't hurt a bit and besides, what else you got to do?"

"Nothing," said Jefferies. "Tomorrow. About noon?"

"At noon, we meet here," said Winters. "John, you bring that big pick up with the camper on it."

"Okay."

Jefferies finished his beer and pulled a buck from his pocket. "Got to go. The old lady has something planned and told me to get home early."

"Only a couple of weeks more," said Winters, "and you won't have to worry about the old lady."

"Couple of weeks, and I'll be sitting on a beach somewhere, watching the girls in their bikinis."

"Tomorrow," Winters reminded him as he headed toward the door.

4

Although they had planned to be on the road by eight in the morning, it wasn't until nine that they pulled out of the parking lot of Davis's apartment building. She hadn't been ready when Collins arrived. She'd met him at the door in her robe looking as if she'd just gotten out of bed, with her hair piled on the top of her head and told him that she'd overslept.

"In the Army, we don't oversleep," Collins had told her. "Men have died and battles have been lost because people have overslept."

"I wasn't planning on a battle today," she said, turning and walking back into her apartment.

Collins followed and then parked himself on the couch in front of the television. While she dressed, he watched the Saturday morning cartoons and wondered why one of the stations couldn't show a movie for the adults who weren't interested in the animated antics of funny animals.

She had reappeared a few minutes later wearing a light colored blouse, short shorts that barely covered her, knee socks and tennis shoes. "How do I look?"

Collins had been amazed by the transformation. During

the week, in uniform, she had looked older and a little dowdy. But now, with her hair down, wearing clothes designed for a younger woman, she looked like a teenager going on a picnic. A young, good looking woman.

"Any time," said Collins.

"You didn't tell me what you thought."

Collins shrugged and tried to remember that he was a captain and she was a sergeant. The military had written regulations about the conduct of officers and enlisted personnel, especially when the officer was male and the enlisted soldier was female. But looking at her, it was difficult to remember. Next to impossible.

"You look great."

"Worth the wait without a lecture for oversleeping?" she asked.

"I wasn't lecturing you. Just gently reminding you that as soldiers, we are geared to time tables."

"Not on dates," she said.

Collins felt a knife thrust into his stomach. An icy cold lump that vibrated there. It wasn't supposed to be a real date. It was during the day and dates happened at night. There was no money being spent for a restaurant or movie tickets. He was providing the transportation and she was providing the food. That was how he had rationalized his acceptance of the invitation. Two soldiers, friends, spending some time together off-duty. Buddies going for a beer. It was a lot of things, but it wasn't a date. Of that he was sure.

He decided the best course was to ignore the fact she thought of it as a date. He'd just think of it as an outing to search for treasure that didn't exist. A day spent with a buddy from the office.

But then she'd come out of the kitchen with a fancy basket. She set it on the table and insisted on showing him

everything that was in it, from the plastic plates and silver-
ware strapped to the top, to the red and white checkered
cloth, to the food and wine that filled it. Cold fried
chicken, deviled eggs, potato salad, bananas and apples,
and two bottles of wine, one red and one white.

"Potato salad'll go bad quickly in the heat. Maybe the
eggs too."

"Nope," she'd said, grinning. Pulling aside the napkins,
she pointed out the small ice holder. "If we keep the lid
down, the inside will stay cold for five or six hours. Nothing will go bad."

"Then, if you're ready, let's go."

They'd walked to the parking lot, stored the basket in
the trunk, and driven out onto the street. They'd left the
town, the people just coming out on the Saturday chores,
driven south toward Sierra Vista and then east.

As they did, Davis looked back at the fort and asked,
"Aren't we going on post?"

"Nope," said Collins. "Won't do any good to look there.
First, I figure the Army has already done that. Searched
until they were sure that no gold was hidden on the post.
Second, even if we found something, the Army'd take it all
away from us anyway."

She thought about that and then asked, "Isn't that like
the man who was searching for his lost wallet at night, not
where he'd dropped it but near the lamp because the light
was so much better?"

Collins turned onto a dirt road and said, "Sort of. The
difference is, we don't know exactly where the treasure
might be located, and we believe the Army has already
searched their land carefully. Therefore the best place for
us to search is off post."

"And you have a location in mind?"

Collins slowed for a curve and then stepped on the gas

again. "After we talked, I went back and examined some of the old records. Checked to see what I could learn about the treasure and the location of it. Given all that, and after looking at the maps, I decided that if you were serious about looking for the gold, this would be the best location."

They came to a bend in the road and there was a wide place on the shoulder not far from it. Collins pulled over and stopped. He consulted the map that was lying on the seat and then pointed. "Out in that direction," he said, "is where we want to go."

"There's nothing out there," she said.

"What'd you expect? I think that those low hills, about a mile from here might be the place to look."

"I don't know," said Davis. "Can't we get closer than this?"

"I don't want to drive overland. Tears up the desert, destroys the vegetation, the little there is, and leaves ruts in the sand."

"So we walk?"

"It's only a mile or mile and one half. Then we'll have a chance to search among those hills and the arroyos. If there is a cave entrance, or anything like that, it'll be concealed over there."

"You're sure?"

Collins laughed. "If I was sure, I would be out of the Army, driving a new car, and out here by myself so that I wouldn't have to share the money."

"Then you're not sure."

"I'm telling you that to the best of my ability and knowledge, that is where the treasure is hidden. In the hills over there."

Davis threw open her door and said, "Then let's go get it."

Jefferies met the others as they had discussed the day before. Winters, wearing dirty work clothes, was sitting on the hood of his car, an old Ford LTD. Boyle, in faded blue jeans and a torn T-shirt, was standing there, a hand to his forehead to shield his eyes. He was watching Winters drink a beer from a bottle.

As Jefferies got out of his car, he leaned against the roof and the top of the door, and looked over at the other two. He glanced at his watch. "I'm here."

"And late."

"Not much."

Winters finished his beer and threw the bottle at a fifty-five gallon drum at the corner of the building. It hit the rim and shattered.

"You drive," said Winters.

"Why?" asked Jefferies.

"Because you know where the bodies are and this way we don't have to hassle with you giving instructions and one of us trying to follow them."

"How's about a beer first?" said Jefferies.

"Shit," said Winters. "Let's just get going."

Jefferies sat back down and pulled the door shut. He waited as Winters opened the passenger door and pulled the seat forward so that Boyle could climb in the back.

As he shut the door, Winters looked at Jefferies. "Where's your jeep?"

"Left it home," said Jefferies. "Didn't want the jeep seen out there two days in a row."

"Good idea," said Winters. "You've finally stopped thinking with your butt and begun to use your head."

Jefferies started the engine and pulled out onto the high-way. Now he headed north and the west, back toward Sierra Vista. He drove in silence, the radio having stopped working long before and since it was his wife's car, he hadn't bothered to fix it. Neither Winters nor Boyle spoke.

For a few moments, Jefferies wondered if they were angry because he'd shot the hikers rather than just chasing them off. He could have done that easily. All he'd have to have done would have been to come flying off the hills in his jeep, honking at them as he aimed at them, and scared them. They'd have run away and not returned.

But maybe that wouldn't have been enough. And they might have been curious about it. Maybe they would have come back later, when he wasn't around. Maybe they'd have found the cave. Maybe they'd have told someone about the strange man in a jeep and those people would come out figuring something must be hidden out there.

No, he told himself silently, the only thing he could do was kill them.

"How far?" asked Winters.

"Couple of miles."

They pulled off the highway, onto a dirt road. Jefferies stepped on the gas, taking off. A plume of dust rose behind them. Jefferies slid around a corner, the rear fishtailing. He glanced at Winters who sat leaning back, against the seat and the door, one hand braced against the dashboard.

"Hey," said Boyle. "Slow it down."

Jefferies shot him a glance in the rearview mirror, and then ignored him. He spun the wheel, slipped around an-other corner and then glanced up in the mirror again. The dust hung behind them like an incoming fog.

Finally he stepped on the brake, locking the wheels as they slid to a halt. The dust caught them, wrapped them and then drifted past them. Jefferies backed up and turned

down a side road. The road seemed to fade away. It
changed from a gravel to a dirt track and then to two lines
in the sand. They came out on a small hill that overlooked
the desert floor.

"Down there," said Jefferies.

Collins got out of the car, walked around to the trunk
and opened it. He stood there, looking at the basket and
thought about carrying it two miles across the sand. No
problem to carry it down the stairs in the air conditioned
apartment building, and no problem to carry it across the
parking lot at nine o'clock in the morning because it wasn't
very hot yet. But carrying it two miles, across the desert
with the sun hanging overhead just didn't appeal to him.

Davis got out and put on the cowboy hat she'd brought
with her. She approached the trunk and asked, "Is there
something wrong?"

"I'm not thrilled with carrying the picnic basket," said
Collins.

"Then don't. We can leave it here, take a walk and
return to the car when we get hungry."

"All right," said Collins. He reached up with both hands
and slammed down the trunk. He walked around to the
door, leaned in and retrieved his map. He plucked a pistol
belt from the back seat. It held three canteens, a hunting
knife, small survival kit, snake bite kit and a first aid kit.
He buckled it on and then stood up. Finally he rolled the
window down an inch or two and closed the door.

Davis did the same on the other side. Then, before they
moved off, Collins spread the map out. Pointing at the
distant landmarks, he said, "According to one story, a prospector was searching around here and his mule stumbled
into a hole. The whole mule fell in, breaking its leg. The
prospector jumped down, figuring he'd put the poor beast

out of its misery and saw, in a shaft of light, a reflection. He walked deeper into the cave and came to the gold, stacked neatly on the cave's floor, almost as if it was in a bank vault."

"I've heard that one," said Davis.

"He talked about landmarks," said Collins. "I think that the point he referred to is about two or three miles off. A good, long, hot walk."

"Then let's go."

Collins folded his map and stuffed it in the hip pocket of his pants. He took a compass from his pocket, sighted and said, "All right. We walk straight to those low hills."

Davis adjusted her pistol belt which held only two canteens and a first aid kit. She'd had trouble fixing it so that it would fit her. She was almost too small to wear it.

"Let's go," said Collins impatiently.

They walked down into the ditch at the side of the road, then up to the barbed wire fence. Collins stepped on the bottom strand and pulled up on the one next to the bottom so that Davis could climb through easily without cutting herself. As she bent to slip into the field, he watched as the fabric of her shorts stretched tight and pulled up slightly. Quickly he averted his eyes, reminding himself that she was an enlisted soldier under his direct supervision and that he was playing with fire even being out of the office with her.

She turned then, grabbed the wire and held the strands apart from him. He followed her through and then stood. He wiped the sweat from his face and said, "Going to be a hot one."

"We've plenty of water."

"Right."

They moved off together, walking in the soft sand, avoiding the stunted bushes. Collins found it hard shortening his stride to match hers, but didn't say a word about it. He tried to keep his eyes off her legs, and off the sweat-stains that were turning her cotton blouse transparent. The longer they were in the heat the more obvious it was that she hadn't bothered with a bra.

And he tried to keep his mind off the fact that she was walking closer to him than she had to, or that she'd sat close to him in the car. Had he not put the maps in the center of the seat, she might have been sitting right next to him, which was fine for teenagers on their way to the drive-in but not for military personnel.

Now they were walking across the desert, out of sight of the road, no one around for miles, and he was aware of her as he'd never been in the office. He saw her not as a ser-geant in the United States Army, but as a woman, and that was beginning to scare him because regulations could smash him, and he'd find his butt in South Vietnam dodg-ing bullets and Viet Cong instead of female sergeants.

He moved away from her, but it did no good. She fol-lowed him until her hip was only inches from his and he was convinced he could feel the heat of her body, even through the heat of the desert day.

As they continued on, he was suddenly aware of buz-zards in the air, high overhead, circling like fighters with a target below them. He glanced up at them, shaded his eyes with a hand and looked out over the desert.

"They really circle something dead?" asked Davis.

"Dead or dying," said Collins.

"I thought that was something invented in Hollywood because it looked good in the movies. The circling buz-zards would lead the wagonmaster to the lost wagon, or lead the cavalry to the site of the massacre."

"Probably a range steer that fell and broke a leg and is dying of thirst."

"Maybe we'd better go see," said Davis. "We might be able to help."

"I doubt it," said Collins.

"We could go look."

Collins shrugged. "We could go look."

They turned slightly, angling toward the west, where it seemed the buzzards were located. They stopped once and Collins cupped both hands around his eyes, trying to spot whatever was drawing the buzzards.

They continued on, until they could see something lying on the sand. A dark shape a hundred yards away. Directly over it were the buzzards.

Collins pointed. "There. Looks like whatever it was is dead now."

"We'd better be sure," said Davis, her voice high and tight and strained.

Collins wasn't sure that he wanted to see the remains of a steer or whatever, after the buzzards and other scavengers had gotten at it. There'd be flies and a stench that could knock over a bull. But then, Davis seemed convinced that it was a wounded animal that needed their help.

"We'll take a quick look," said Collins.

"Okay."

They walked forward, their pace nowhere as fast as it had been. Neither wanted to see the animal, but neither wanted to chicken out. They were committed to finding the body of whatever lay out there.

As they approached, the shape separated until they could see there were two things lying there and when they got closer, Davis said, "I still can't quite make it out."

And then, suddenly, Collins knew what they were looking at. He'd seen enough movies, read enough books. He knew. Under his breath, he said, "Oh my God."

"What? What is it?"

But neither of them stopped. They walked on until Collins could see the shape of the bodies and could see the wounds to them. He could see the darkness of the stains that was the dried blood and he could tell that one was male and the other female and both were dead.

Suddenly Davis stopped and then fell to her knees. She wrapped her arms around her belly, as if she was about to be sick and said, "Oh God oh God oh God."

"You wait here," said Collins.

She glanced up at him, her eyes wet, her face pale. She nodded dumbly.

Collins moved forward until he was no more than fifteen feet from the bodies. Both were nude. The man had been shot once in the chest, the bullet hole evident. Animals had gotten at some of the softer tissues, tearing at them. If it hadn't been for the thickness at the waist and the hair on the legs, he might not have known it was a man.

He tore his eyes away from that body and looked at the other. Part of the head was missing, the result of the bullet in the face. He could see her brain, a gray-green mass that was baking in the desert sun. She'd been shot in the shoulder once so that the bullet to the head must have been to make sure she was dead.

Collins felt his stomach flip over and thought he was going to lose his breakfast. The sound of the flies, the stink of the rotting meat, the sight of the ripped bodies got to him. He turned his head, closed his eyes and forced himself to swallow. Cold sweat suddenly took the place of that he'd worked up walking across the desert. His head spun and as he opened his eyes, the landscape was suddenly out of focus, tilting right and left as if they were in the center of the ocean.

"Jason," said Davis, her voice shaky. "Jason. Let's get out of here."

He nodded but didn't speak right away. Finally he looked at her and walked slowly back toward her. "Yes. We've got to get out of here. We don't want to destroy the evidence." His voice was hollow and his eyes vacant.

"What happened to them?"

For a moment he didn't say a word. He was in a world of his own, but then he shook himself. "Someone shot them. Shot them both."

"Why? Why would anyone shoot two people like that?" she asked. She tried to keep from looking at the bodies, but couldn't stop herself. She had to see the bullet holes, the blood and the gore. Just for an instant. Just to see what it really looked like.

Collins didn't have an answer for her question. It was impossible to define the reasons people would commit murder. Especially out in the desert where there was nothing of value to steal. And then suddenly he knew. He could think of two hundred million reasons for someone to commit murder out there. Suddenly he was frightened. He could feel the crosshairs centered on his back, and he could hear the quiet breathing of the hidden sniper who was about to drop the hammer on him as he had done to the two other people.

He grabbed Davis under the arm and jerked her to her feet. "Yes," he said, his voice suddenly husky with fear. "Let's get the hell out of here."

5

Lying on the hot sand of the ridge that looked down on the open plain, Jefferies, Winters, and Boyle watched in horror as two more people began the trek toward the cave opening. Using binoculars that Jefferies took from the backseat, they studied the two people, a man and a woman. They watched as the man used a compass and checked his map.

Jefferies turned to the side and whispered, "They're searching for the treasure."

"So what?" asked Winters, his voice unnaturally loud.

"Quiet," hissed Jefferies.

"Why? They're too far to hear us and even if they do, so what?"

Jefferies didn't know what to say. He didn't want anyone walking anywhere near the hidden entrance to his cave. He knew it was unlikely that anyone would stumble across the entrance. It had been difficult to find in the first place and they'd made changes to hide it better. But there were suddenly too many people wandering around on the one stretch of desert that could lead them right to the cave.

"We've got to stop them," said Jefferies.

"No. We've got to leave them alone," said Winters. "Then we've got to make plans to get the gold out of there and take it somewhere else."

"How?" asked Boyle.

"I don't know, yet," said Winters. "I do know that we can't shoot those two people. If four people suddenly disappear, there are going to be questions. Anyway there are going to be hundreds of people out searching."

"Oh shit," said Jefferies.

"What?"

"They've changed direction. They're walking straight at the bodies now."

Winters took the binoculars and focused on the people. He nodded and said, "You're right. They know that there is something wrong over there."

"We've got to kill them now," said Jefferies.

"No!" said Winters.

"But they'll find the bodies and go to the sheriff. He'll come out here and we'll have a couple of hundred people roaming all over the place."

"Calm down," said Winters. "You've got to remember that the cave has been there for years, centuries, and no one found it. It'll be safe. And we can't shoot everyone whose walking around out on the desert."

"So what do we do?"

"Wait for them to get out and then go collect the bodies just as we planned. We'll bury them somewhere else. Sheriff'll come out, say that he doesn't see any bodies and that'll be the end of it."

"They'll know we moved them."

Winters nodded in the direction of the two people and said, "They'll know, but the sheriff won't. If he's got no missing persons report, he'll let it slide for now. He'll go home, have a beer and watch the game on the TV.

What we don't want to do is panic and shoot anyone else."

Winters raised the binoculars to his eyes. Finally he said, "They've found the bodies now." He laughed. "Looks like they're both going to be sick."

"Let's just kill them," said Jefferies. His voice was higher now. He was fidgeting, as if the hot sand was bothering him. He was like the little kid in school who suddenly had to go to the bathroom.

"Quit being stupid. Now there, see, they're getting out. Almost running back the way they came."

"To get the sheriff."

Winters handed the binoculars to Jefferies. "Now, here's what we do. Hurry down there and pick up the bodies and carry them up here. Boyle, you'll remain behind down there hiding all evidence of our movements. Kick sand over the blood stains or anything else that suggests there was someone killed there. Then, move back here, wiping out our footprints with a bush. Make it hard for them. Make the desert look like it did before we went walking around on it."

"Okay," said Boyle.

Jefferies held the binoculars to his eyes. "They're out of sight now."

"You got anything in the car to carry the bodies in?"

"Trash bags," said Jefferies.

"Get them."

Jefferies slipped to the rear and then stood up. He hurried to the car and opened the trunk, taking out the trash bags. He also spotted a broom and figured that it would be useful to Boyle.

As he approached them, Winters said, "Let's go."

They hurried down the slope, to the flat and then across the desert floor. They reached the bodies and Jefferies pulled out one of the trash bags.

Looking at the bodies, Winters shook his head. "You didn't have to mutilate them."

"I didn't," said Jefferies. He was staring at the dead woman. Looking at her and wishing again that he hadn't had to kill her.

"Give me that," said Winters. He opened it up and then looked from it to the body as if trying to figure out the best way to cram it in.

Jefferies said, "Put the feet in one and the head in the other and tie them together."

Winters crouched down and slipped the bag over the head and shoulders of the man. "Help me," he said.

Jefferies crouched and lifted the feet, jamming them into the bag, pulling it up to the man's waist. Using the twist ties, he pushed them through the plastic material to hook the top bag to the bottom.

"That'll do it."

"Now the girl," said Winters.

While they worked to put her body in the bag, Boyle scraped at the sand with the broom, hiding footprints, blood and bits of flesh torn from the bodies by the scavengers.

Winters struggled to pick up the body of the man. Rigor mortis had stiffened the body so that it was hard to handle. Picking it caused the gases to explode through the rips in the flesh.

"Christ, this guy is ripe."

Jefferies cradled the woman in his arms. The stiff, unyielding flesh made it difficult to lift her but once he'd done that, he was able to carry her. He started off across the desert. At the foot of the gentle slope that climbed to the ridge, he stopped and slipped to one knee, balancing the body but refusing to put it down.

Sweat soaked him and dripped down his face. It

splashed into his eyes, stinging them. He blinked rapidly but that didn't seem to help. He turned his head and tried to wipe the sweat on his shoulder.

Winters was struggling with the man, his feet sinking into the soft sand as he fought to keep from falling. His legs pumped like the running back struggling against the whole defensive line as he tried to reach the goal line.

Taking a deep breath, Jefferies stood up and began the climb. With the awkward weight of the dead girl in his arms, he moved slowly. The breath rasped in his throat and he felt like he'd sprinted a mile.

Halfway up the hill, he slipped and fell, landing on the girl. There was a rush of air and then a quiet groan. Jefferies leaped back like he'd been burned. He fell back, on his butt, a look of horror on his face.

"She's not dead," he said quietly. Then he screamed it. "She's not dead."

Winters had reached the top of the rise and had dropped his burden on the sand. He was bend over, breathing hard. He turned slowly and looked down at Jefferies.

"Of course she's dead."

"She said something."

Winters stomped down the hill to the body. He kicked it once. "She's dead. Period."

"I heard her."

"Gases in the body you asshole."

Jefferies looked first at Winters and then back at the plastic bag wrapped woman. His face was pale and his eyes were wide.

"You sure?"

"Jesus!" Winters looked toward the sky as if seeking heavenly guidance. He grabbed the body and lifted it. He stood there, staring at Jefferies. "If she wasn't dead, she wouldn't be stiff."

Slowly Jefferies climbed to his feet. "Yeah. That's right, I guess."

They both worked their way to the top of the ridge. Boyle was following, using the broom to sweep away their footprints. As he reached the top where Winters was trying to stuff the dead man in the trunk of the car he stopped sweeping.

"Unless they look real close, no one's going to see anything."

"Okay," said Winters. He picked up the girl and tried to push her into the trunk, but she wouldn't quite fit. He stepped back and raised a foot, stomping on her trash bag covered body. There was a snap as the bones in her legs broke.

"Oh God," said Boyle.

"Shut up," snapped Winters.

Jefferies grabbed the trunk lid and slammed it down. It didn't catch the first time and he had to hit it again.

"Now," said Winters, dusting the palms of his hands together. "We get out of here and dump the bodies."

"Where?"

"In Mexico, of course. Throw everyone way off the trail."

"Good," said Jefferies. "Real good."

Tynan was leaning back with his eyes closed as the radio played and air conditioning hummed. King was driving, having taken over after lunch and she was burning up the highway. The speed limit was seventy-five and she was holding it just under eighty.

Tynan opened an eye and looked out at the bleak landscape. Sand, stunted bushes and a little grass, here and there. The dominant feature was the huge yellow signs every mile or two that promised a variety to things to entice the driver from the highway and into the upcoming trading post-restaurant-museum featuring freaks, curiosities and relics of the past.

"How long those signs been around?"

"Last twenty or thirty miles," said King. "My favorite is the two headed rattlesnake that could bite two victims at once. That might be something to see."

Tynan sat up then. "You can stop if you want. I wouldn't mind a Coke or something."

"It's still fifty miles away."

"Then it's something to look forward to," said Tynan.

They drove in silence for a few moments and then King said, "You don't think much about this idea, do you?"

"What am I supposed to think?" He laughed. "I find it hard to believe that you supposedly well educated people would fall for an old fairy tale about treasure hidden in the desert southwest. Seems to me that these rumors would have been started long ago by land developers and swindlers to get the gullible to leave the safe confines of New York, Chicago or St. Louis to risk their lives for a treasure that doesn't exist."

"We've proof," said King.

"You have some old documents that suggest the conquistadors hid some gold north of the valley of Mexico. You don't have any real proof that they hid the treasure in Arizona."

"We know that they got that far north. Spanish explorers roamed through this whole area. They were followed by the monks who wanted to convert the Indians for the church."

"Doesn't mean that they hid treasure," said Tynan.

"No, it doesn't. But they were here. And you forget about the Tayopa trove in the Sierra Madres. The Tayopa was one of three mines that were so close together that a dog barking in one of them could be heard in the other two."

Tynan rubbed his face and stared out at the highway. "Again you're talking about a lost treasure or lost mine, but there is nothing to suggest the legends are true. Not to mention the fact the mines are in the Sierra Madres of northern Mexico, not in Arizona."

"But one of the mines was found," said King. "And the existence of the Tayopa is documented. The Guaynopa was found and showed signs of having been a major mine. Spanish records show that a great deal of treasure was taken from the mine in the Seventeenth Century."

"Fine," said Tynan. "I believe there were mines scattered throughout the area. I know that the Spanish enslaved the Indians and forced them to work the mines. I know that they shipped millions, billions of dollars to Spain."

"And some of the ships went down in storms. Records exist showing that there are millions lying on the bottom of the ocean."

"I believe that too," said Tynan.

"Then why do you reject the idea of treasures on land?" she asked.

"Because there is never any proof and there isn't the intervention of nature to jerk the treasure from the hands of those who hold it."

King slowed behind a truck and then pulled out to pass it. She stepped on the gas, running the speed up to ninety, and then slipped back, slowing.

"The Tayopa is different," she said. "The records of the gold dug out of it exist in Spain. The Jesuits didn't want to give twenty percent of their treasure to the Spanish crown, so they refused to ship anything to Spain."

"Fine."

"They stockpiled it in the Tayopa. Conservative estimates put the value of the treasure at twenty-three million dollars. Given today's prices, that might be more."

"Still doesn't prove a thing. You had the Jesuits around the mine. They knew where it was and now suddenly it's lost."

King laughed. "It wasn't quite that easy. The Apaches also roamed that area and during a fiesta in 1640 or '50, or something like that, attacked the village killing everyone. They then sealed the entrance to the mine and kept everyone out of the region for over a century."

Now Tynan laughed. "Sure."

"The other two mines have been found," insisted King. "Bits of gold, and the small artifacts have been found, but the main treasure is still missing."

"All right," said Tynan. "Even if I accept the Lost Tayopa as a real place with real treasure in it, that doesn't put two hundred million at Fort Huachuca."

"But it establishes the precedence," said King. "It proves that Jesuits, who established missions throughout the desert southwest, also searched for gold, silver and other precious metals. And it proves that when they found them, they hid them from the Spanish crown."

"It's a wild goose chase," said Tynan.

"No. The treasure is there. We know it's there. We just have to make an effort to find it."

"Sure," said Tynan. He pointed at the road sign and asked, "You want to see the two headed rattlesnake."

"Changing the subject?" she asked.

"No. I'm just hungry again."

"Then by all means, let's stop and see the two headed rattlesnake."

6

Collins sat in the car for a moment, outside the sheriff's office and stared down, toward the speedometer. He wiped the sweat from his face and glanced over at Davis. She still looked as if she was going to be sick at any moment.

"You can stay here, if you want," he said.

She shook her head. "No. I want to go in."

"You have your ID card with you?"

She touched the purse she had carried with her and said, "Yes, I think so."

"Then let's go and remember, this isn't going to be very easy."

"I know." She used the handle and pushed open the door. Heat boiled in, overwhelming the cool from the air conditioner, but she didn't notice it.

Collins climbed out the other side and stood there looking at the low brick building with the radio antennas on it. There was a double door that led inside, but the glass was tinted, making it difficult to see the interior. As they walked toward the doors, Collins wondered if they shouldn't have reported to the Provost Marshall first. The Army would have no jurisdiction over the incident, but the

Provost Marshall might want to learn about it first since he and Davis were military.

But then they were through the door and on the inside which was brightly lighted. There was green tile on the floor, cinderblock walls painted a light canary yellow. In front of him was a desk raised off the floor, set behind a partial wall of cinderblocks and a glass cage. A burly man was sitting there, reading something and paying no attention to the people who came in the front.

Collins stepped up, waited a moment and then said, "I'd like to report a murder."

The deputy glanced up, down and closed whatever he was reading. "Now, what was that?"

"We found the bodies of two people in the desert. Shot," he said.

"You're sure?"

Collins glanced at the deputy and then toward Davis. Finally he said, "You're fairly calm about this."

"We get all kinds of reports in here all the time and it just makes sense to check them out before we go running off into the desert to look at the skeleton of a range cow or a dead deer."

"These were people. Man and a woman. Both had been shot sometime in the recent past, I'd say."

"You got some ID?" asked the deputy.

Collins pulled out his wallet and showed the deputy his green military ID card.

"Wait right there, Captain," said the deputy. "I'll get someone out there to take your statement."

"Shouldn't we head back out to the site?"

"Naw. Bodies aren't going anywhere and they'll still be dead when we get there. Get the preliminaries out of the way and then take a trip."

Collins shrugged, surprised the deputy didn't get excited about the double murder, or didn't call the sheriff. He just told them to wait for another deputy to come out and take their statements.

A door to the right opened and a man stuck his head out. "Captain Collins?"

Collins moved toward the door, Davis right behind him. They entered a large open area filled with desks, filing cabinets, brightly lighted and with carpeting on the floor. There were half a dozen men and two women working, some talking on the phone, some hunched over paperwork and two of them talking to a third man who seemed to be a prisoner.

The man led them through the room and pointed to a desk. "Have a seat there. Would either of you like some coffee?"

"No, thank you," said Davis. Collins shook his head.

"Then we're all set. I'm Deputy Lawrence Travis." He held out a hand to be shaken. Collins did it and dropped into the visitor's chair. Davis sat there, staring at the floor as if unaware of what was happening around her.

"Now," said Travis, taking a sheet of paper from the top desk drawer, "why don't you tell me what the problem is?"

"We found two bodies in the desert east of here. Shot. The woman twice and the man once. Scavengers had gotten at them and chewed them up a little."

"You're sure they were human."

Collins glanced at Davis and then nodded at Travis. "Completely sure."

Travis looked at Davis and asked, "What did you see?"

For a moment she was quiet but she did look up. Quietly she said, "They were both dead."

"Any idea who they were?"

Collins said, "We didn't touch anything. Both were

naked so we don't have a clue. I just made sure they were dead and then we came here."

Travis made a notation on his form and then said, "I guess the thing to do is drive out there and have a look. Then we can decide what we need to do."

"Maybe she should wait here," said Collins.

"No. Let's all drive out there and take a look."

"You have a jeep or something to drive across the desert? The bodies are a mile or so from the road."

"I think we can accommodate you," said Travis, standing. "Any time you're ready."

With two bodies in the trunk, Jefferies was not the speed demon he'd been. The last thing he wanted was to be pulled over by some anxious highway patrolman and then have to explain the stench coming from the trunk. That wouldn't do. So he had slowed down to the speed limit and tried to remember the various traffic rules that he had forgotten.

Boyle sat in the back, hunched forward, as if trying to talk to the men in the front, but he was just trying to put more distance between himself and bodies. He'd opened the windows even though Jefferies had the air conditioner on. Jefferies said nothing about trying to cool the outside, because he was convinced he could smell the rotting flesh too.

"We're never going to get that smell out of the trunk," said Jefferies.

"Gasoline will mask it," said Winters. "Nothing wrong with the odor of gasoline in a car. Natural thing."

They reached the main highway and turned south. As they drove along, Jefferies said, "It's not going to be easy to get across the border."

"Then we won't," said Winters. "Hell, we can dump

them close to it. That'll look as if someone raided across the border. It doesn't matter, just as long as no one is looking for them back where you shot them."

Jefferies took one hand off the wheel and rubbed his face hard. He wiped the sweat on his soiled shirt. He reached down for the radio and then remembered that it was broken.

It was the bodies in the trunk. They were making him nervous. He didn't want to get caught with them. He didn't want to go to jail. The creeps deserved what they got because they shouldn't have been fucking around in the desert, but that wouldn't be the way the police saw it. They'd just see them as victims of a crime of murder and he'd be in jail with no chance to spend his money.

"Once we dump the bodies," he said, raising his voice over the noise of the wind whipping in the windows. "Once we dump the bodies, maybe we should talk about getting the gold out of there."

"We got a problem there," said Winters, speaking patiently. "I told you before that it's illegal for private citizens to own gold. How you going to explain to anyone where you got a bar of gold? There'll be questions asked. Lots of questions that can't be answered."

"I know that," said Jefferies, "but I thought you was getting it out of the country. Into Mexico."

Winters looked a the man and shook his head. "You just don't listen. I've got to move carefully. Those bandits will cut your throat for the boots you wear. Have to move slowly and let them know that killing me will shut off the supply. Got to convince them that there is more coming later. Keep the carrot on the stick way out in front of them."

"I don't like them getting forty percent," said Boyle.

"Shit man, who cares?" said Winters. "When you've

got a hundred million or more, forty percent is nothing. We each get twenty million. So who cares? How many cars can you drive anyway?"

"Still," said Boyle.

"Still, shit," said Winters. "You can do better, you do better. Right now it isn't doing us shit in the ground. Sixty percent of a hundred million is better than a hundred percent of nothing."

"When you put it that way," said Boyle.

"Oh shit," said Jefferies. "Cop coming up behind us."

"Don't get panicky," said Winters. "He sees you sweating and looking nervous, he's going to pull you over. He sees you sitting there nice and calm, he's going to ignore you."

Jefferies turned and put both hands on the wheel. He sat up straight, like a kid in school. He focused his eyes on the road in front of him.

"Relax," hissed Winters.

The cop pulled up beside them. Jefferies refused to look for a moment and then turned his head. He saw the cop looking at him and didn't know what to do. Finally he nodded politely and turned his attention back to the road.

The police car pulled ahead of them and then sped off. As it disappeared over the top of a hill, Jefferies fell back against the seat and sighed. "Christ, that was close."

"You handled it just fine," said Winters. "Remember what you did. Glanced at him and then back at the road. Just right. Told him that you knew he was there and that you didn't care."

"I'll be glad when this is over," said Jefferies.

"Yeah," said Winters, "I think we've pressed our luck about as far as we can. Let's take the next dirt road and see where it leads us."

Jefferies slowed down. They topped the hill and the police car was sitting by the side of the highway.

"He's looking for speeders," said Winters, but he didn't sound quite as sure of himself as before.

Jefferies glanced at the speedometer and then slowed slightly so that he was on the speed limit. They approached the car, but the officer didn't seem interested in them at all. As they drove by, Jefferies looked up at the rearview miror, expecting the lights to come on and the police cruiser to pull out. That didn't happen.

As they crested the next hill and the police car was gone, Winters said, "Just looking for speeders."

Jefferies spotted a side road and turned down it. When they were out of sight of the road he stopped, letting the dust settle behind him. The police car was still apparently sitting at the side of the road, waiting for speeders. Convinced that they were not being followed, he shifted into drive and began to move along the dirt road.

They climbed a few hills, crossed more than one arroyo and then came to an old adobe building with walls that were falling down and a roof that had caved in. Behind it was the foundation of a barn and what looked to be a well.

Winters pointed and said, "That's perfect."

Jefferies stopped the car and sat there looking. No one had been around in weeks, though there were a few beer cans lying on the ground and the remains of a fire.

"What's perfect?"

"The well in back. If it's deep, and around here it would have to be, we can throw the bodies down there and they'll never be found."

Jefferies turned off the engine and got out. He stood there, a hand up to shade his eyes. There was no one in the desert around them. The land looked as it had a hundred years ago, maybe a thousand years ago. Other than the adobe house and well, nothing that suggested humans had ever walked the land around them.

He walked over toward the house and looked in. Rotting timber and a dirty odor. As he searched it, Winters got out of the car and headed toward the well.

Jefferies joined him. It had been boarded over at one point, but the wood was gray and weak. He reached down, grabbed at a corner and lifted. With a quiet popping, the wood gave. From the darkness below he heard a sound like dry leaves blowing on a fall breeze.

"Snakes," said Winters.

"Oh, Christ," snapped Jefferies jumping to the rear. "Not snakes."

Winters took a lighter from his pocket but the weak flame did nothing to chase the gloom. He pulled at a couple more boards, but still couldn't see the bottom of the well.

"Let's get the bodies and get rid of them."

"Right," said Jefferies. He hurried to the car and then around to the driver's side for the keys. Snagging them from the ignition, he walked to the rear and opened the trunk. The stench rolled out at him, driving him back.

"Jeez, they smell." He moved closer, bent over but couldn't reach in.

"Hold your breath," suggested Boyle who'd just gotten out of the rear.

"I can't hold my breath and carry a body thirty yards."

Winters, holding his breath, reached into the trunk and snatched the gas can from it. He moved away and opened the can, sprinkling some gas on his handkerchief.

"The odor of gas kills the ability to smell. Tie the rag with some gas on it around your head so the gas is right under your nose and we'll be able to move the bodies."

Jefferies stood there looking dumb. He didn't want to

move. He didn't want to touch the bodies. He just wanted to get into the car and drive off. Instead, he followed Winters' lead, soaking a cloth in gas and using it to paralize his nose.

Together, they lifted the girl's body from the car and carried it toward the well. They dropped her next to it and pried up several of the boards, creating a hole large enough to stuff the body in. They lifted it, tilted it and let it slide down, into the darkness below. As it did, the trash bag over her head pulled free, giving Jefferies a final look at her. He felt nothing as she disappeared, hitting bottom with a dull thud an instant later.

He kicked at the bag so that it would float down, into the well. Noise erupted from it. Rattlesnakes shaking their anger at the sudden intrusion.

"Let's get the man and get the hell out of here," said Winters.

Jefferies noticed that Winters wasn't as confident as he had been. His color was bad and he was shaking. The steel underneath was beginning to sag slightly.

They got the body of the man and disposed of it the same way. Then, standing over the hole, Winters ripped the rag from his face and threw it in. When Jefferies had done the same, he began to put the boards back, concealing the hole as best he could.

Jefferies walked back to the car. He leaned against it, his back to it and to the well. He was facing out so that he was looking into the unblemished desert.

"Too bad about them," said Boyle, misunderstanding Jefferies' mood.

He turned to look at Boyle. "Fuck 'em," he said. "They shouldn't have been out there."

Winters approached the car then, dusting his hands. "Okay, let's get out of here."

"What are we going to do about the gold?" asked Jef-feries. "We can't just leave it there."

"Look," said Winters, "right now I just want to get a shower. I need to clean this stink off me. Then we can get together and decide what to do."

"Then we're heading on back?"

"Yes," said Winters. "To the bar so that Boyle and I can get our cars. I think we'd better meet later so that we can decide what to do."

Jefferies slipped behind the wheel. Boyle had closed the trunk and retrieved the keys. Once everyone was in the car, Jefferies started the engine.

"I'll be glad when all this is over."

"I'll be glad when we're all rich," said Winters.

No one had a response for that.

7

It was mid afternoon when Tynan and King pulled into Bisbee and stopped at a gas station. While the tank was filled, they studied the map. Tynan wanted to push on to Sierra Vista, but King wanted to find a room in Bisbee.

"I don't want to be too close to the site of the treasure," she said.

"Why?"

She shrugged. "I don't know. It just seems like I'm wearing a sign that tells all who want to look that I'm here to find the treasure. The farther away I am, the more unlikely it is that anyone will suspect what I'm doing."

"What difference does it make?" asked Tynan. "People might point and laugh at the latest attempt to find the lost Huachuca treasure, but I doubt that anyone will be out there shooting at you."

The man appeared at the window and told her it came to four dollars for the gas. She shoved the bills out at him and he walked off.

"So what do we do now?" she asked.

"It's your expedition," said Tynan quietly, "I'm just along for the ride."

"In that case, let's find a hotel room. Then I'd like to drive over into the desert where we'll be searching. See if there is anything that stands out."

"If the treasure exists," said Tynan, "and I'm not convinced it does, but in case it does, you're not going to be able to walk right up to the cave entrance. If it was that easy, someone would have done it before."

She started the engine and pulled out, onto the street, looking right and left. As she drove along, she was searching for a quiet motel that looked clean, had a swimming pool and a coffee shop, and free TV.

"You have to remember," said King, "that no one has brought the expertise to the search that we have. The Spanish archives in Seville, and those in Mexico City, have provided us with clues that no one else has. If there is a treasure, we'll find it."

Then suddenly, she shouted, "There." She hit the turn signal.

"What?"

"Our motel." She pulled up under the overhang and looked at the solid double doors. "We'll stay here."

Tynan waited in the car as she went inside. Without the air conditioning in the car, it quickly warmed. He rolled down the window but the dry desert air provided no relief. He was surprised at how hot it was because he had always thought of the dry air as not being as uncomfortable as the humid air. Ninety degrees in Vietnam was enough to overwhelm. But a hundred degrees in Arizona wasn't as bad. No humidity.

But then, a hundred and fifteen was bad anywhere. Humidity could make it worse, but it was still hot. Like an oven. There might be no humidity in an oven, but it was still damned hot. And even if there was no humidity in Arizona, it was hot and uncomfortable.

He got out of the car, his shirt soaked with sweat. It was almost hard to breathe in the oppressive air. He was thinking of abandoning the car for the air conditioning of the motel lobby when King reappeared.

"We're in room one sixteen. Around the back."

They got in the car and drove to the rear of the motel. They left the suitcases in the car and King opened the door. The room was frigid. King moved to turn down the air conditioning as Tynan kicked off his shoes and then stretched out on the bed, his hands laced under his head.

"Now what?"

"We could eat or we could relax for a few moments and then drive over to Sierra Vista."

Tynan rolled to his side and watched her as she checked the bathroom and the sink and then the television, making sure that everything worked as promised.

"We just ate, not fifty miles ago." He grinned, thinking about the tiny museum that held a glass cage with half a dozen rattlesnakes in it, a few stuffed animals that represented the fauna of the desert, a few Indian artifacts and in the back, the skeleton of Geronimo. Neither of them believed that, but King wanted to suggest that the bones be buried. It wasn't right to display the human bones for the amusement of the tourists who stopped in.

There had been a couple of tables up near the front and a grill behind a bar. They had hamburgers and cheeseburgers and could fry some chicken. There were cokes and milk shakes and French fries. They ordered chicken in a basket, French fries and Cokes. When they'd finished, they looked at the rattlesnakes which weren't moving much, at the stuffed animals and then Indian artifacts. Then they'd hit the road to Bisbee.

King finished her search of the room and then went out to the car. She returned carrying her suitcase and her briefcase. She put one down on the floor and opened the other, taking out a map of the local area. Then sitting at the table with its two chairs, she pointed at the map.

"Our information," she said, waiting for Tynan.

Tynan rolled over and forced himself up slowly, off the bed. He took the other chair, sat down and repeated, "Your information."

"Shows that the treasure lies in a cave somewhere in this general area. We think there is access to it from Fort Huachuca, but we don't think that's the only access. Everything we know suggests that the Spanish would not trap themselves in a cave with only a single exit. They'd have an escape hatch if it was at all possible."

"Just what do you know about this?" asked Tynan. "You've spent hours telling me about other treasures, about the Lost Adams and the Lost Dutchman and sunken galleons, but nothing about this treasure."

"We believe that it is a cave-mine complex situated near a small pass. There is an old house, an adobe house, near it, but that will probably be a foundation now if anything at all is visible. There is a cave filled with timbers and miners equipment. Inside the cave will be the gold bullion made in an adobe furnace situated either near the entrance to the cave or just inside it. Then, as happened so often, the Apaches raided and killed everyone."

"Great rumor," said Tynan.

"We have documentation," said King.

"I can document practically anything you'd like to see documented."

King took a deep breath. "You aren't required to participate in the search."

Tynan turned the map around and looked at it. There were names that were reminiscent of the old west. Tucson. Tombstone. Cochise Stronghold. He looked at the Dragoon

Mountains and the Swisshelm Mountains and the Coronado National Forest. And of course, Fort Huachuca.

"So where do you think this fabled cave of Spanish gold is located?"

"I think we'll find an entrance right here, in these low hills and arroyos. Everything suggests that the main entrance is right there."

Tynan looked at it. The area looked so small and so built up on the map but he knew once they got out there, they'd find hundreds of square miles of nothing. Looking at a map in a university and claiming that the gold was somewhere near Fort Huachuca was different than getting out into the desert.

"Any time you're ready," said Tynan, "I'll be glad to follow you."

"So where're the bodies?"

Collins stood next to the sheriff's jeep with the extra wide tires for use on the desert and looked at the ground. Their footprints had seemed to lead right to that area. Everything looked the same, except the bodies were gone.

"They were here," he said.

"Nothing's been here," said Travis.

Collins kicked at the dirt, turning some of it over and said, "Someone moved them. That's obvious."

"No," said Travis. "The only thing obvious is that nothing happened out here."

"They were here," said Collins. He wanted to be firm and didn't want to sound as if he was whining. "And someone came and got them."

"Why?" asked Travis.

"Who knows?"

Travis stood there, his arms folded and sweat staining the tailored khaki shirt of his uniform. "You murder someone and leave the bodies, you don't return the next day or the next week to move them."

"You don't believe us," said Travis.

Travis shook his head. "Nope."

"You think we just blew into your office with a cock and bull story about dead bodies."

"Nope." He waited for a reaction and when there was none, said, "I think you thought you saw the bodies. I think you thought you saw them right here. I don't think you saw humans and I don't think they were here."

"So we just wasted your time."

"Nope. It's our job to check these things out. I will tell you though, that if I thought you were making this up for whatever reason, I'd file charges."

"Somehow that doesn't make me feel much better."

Travis moved toward the jeep. "You coming?"

"Don't you think we should look around a little first? Since we're out here anyway."

"There's nothing to look for here."

Collins crouched and looked at the sand. He brushed at it with his fingers, looking for something that would prove that he was right. Finally he stood up and walked in a small circle, his eyes on the sand.

"Time's wasting," said Travis, "and I'm going to miss the game."

Collins expanded his circle, trying to find anything that would prove he'd seen two bodies.

"It's not getting any cooler out here," said Travis. "Besides, there have been no reports of anyone missing, or rather a couple missing. If there were, we'd be more interested, but no one can just disappear."

"Transients," said Collins.

"No car. No reports of an abandoned car. Nothing."

Collins stopped and took off his hat. He scratched his head. "It was right here. It had to be."

"But there's nothing here now," said Travis. "The desert plays tricks. Makes you think you see things that aren't there."

"I was close enough to touch them. I'm not some mental midget who can't tell the difference between a clump of bushes and a dead human body."

"So where are they?" asked Travis.

Collins could only shrug. "That's the question, isn't it?"

While King studied the map, providing directions, Tynan drove. Up and down dirt roads, first to the west and then to the north and then back to the west. It was almost as if they had instituted a search pattern from the air and were zeroing in on a specific location.

King turned the map around and around, searching for landmarks, for river beds and hills and arroyos, trying to locate their position with the map. Tynan drove slowly, the dust cloud sometimes catching them and wrapping the car, obscuring the desert around them. The air conditioning labored and the radio played rock and roll quietly.

Finally she dropped the map to the floor, kicked it out of the way, stared out the windshield and announced, "I think we're close."

Tynan slowed to a crawl and looked around him. A dirt road bordered on one side by a barbed wire fence. In the distance, to the far south there were the remains of a house. To the north was nothing other than open desert with no power lines cutting across it, no telephone poles and no sign of a fence. A huge barren territory which explained why the speed limits were seventy-five and eighty in parts of the west. There was nothing to hit on the road, and the distances between towns was so great.

"Stop the car," said King.

Tynan did as he was told. He put it in park and then turned to face King. She was looking out her window, toward the north where there were low hills cut by flash flood channels and dry stream beds, some of the walls thirty-five or forty feet high.

"We're very close," she said.

"An hour on dirt roads and we're about to drop in on a treasure that has alluded treasure hunters for a couple of centuries?"

"I told you, we've done our research. We're not a bunch of dummies who heard there was something out here somewhere. We've limited our search zone."

"Now what?"

"I suppose the sand is too soft to drive on," she said.

"We'll need a jeep or something. Other than that, we can walk. Those hills aren't more than a mile or a mile and half from here."

"So let's go."

Tynan grabbed her arm. "Wait a minute. You don't just go wandering out in the desert without a little planning. We'll want to take a canteen or two with us. We'll want a knife, snake bite kit and a couple of hats to keep the sun off our heads to prevent sunstroke."

"Why didn't you say something earlier?"

Tynan laughed. "Why didn't you tell me you were planning to roam around in the desert?"

"Okay. We'll return to town, buy the things you mentioned and then come back out here."

"Or wait until tomorrow morning so that we'll have the full day."

"Jeez," said King. "More wasted time."

"Not that much. We can also check the maps closely now that you think you've found the location. I can see about renting a jeep. A few hours spent thinking this thing through will keep us from wasting more time."

"We could look around for an hour," said King. "An hour won't hurt."

"You're not going to find it in an hour," said Tynan.

"How do you know?"

Tynan pointed at the map. "You have the entrance to the cave or mine or whatever marked on there? The exact location?"

She looked at the map, studying it carefully. Finally she said, "Not the exact location."

"Then an hour isn't going to do us any good. Let's go back and plan this out."

"Maybe we could rent a plane."

"Why?"

"We could cover more territory that way."

Tynan shook his head. "Are we going to be able to spot the cave entrance from the air? Are there clues to its location that will be visible from the air?"

"Probably not," said King.

"Then we don't need a plane."

"Okay," she snapped. "But I want to get out of the car."

Tynan turned off the engine. "But we're not going to stray too far out into the desert. It'll kill you quicker than the jungle."

King opened the door and got out. She moved to the very edge of the road and put her hands up to shade her eyes. She spotted a plume of dust coming at them.

"Hey! What's that?"

Tynan walked around the front of the car and stood beside her. "Someone in a jeep. Coming at us."

She turned on him. "You see. We've got to hurry. There are others out there searching."

"I doubt that," said Tynan.

They stood watching the jeep as it crossed the desert. Before it got to the road, it changed direction, coming at them. As it approached, Tynan realized that it was a police vehicle and not casual treasure hunters who had read the same material that King and her people had read.

"Sheriff's deputies," said Tynan.

"What are they doing out here?"

"I think we're about to find out."

The jeep climbed up to the road and turned toward them. It pulled in directly in front of their car. The man in uniform who was driving got out and came for them. He looked at Tynan, then King, and asked, "What are you people doing out here?"

"Sightseeing."

"Not good enough," said the deputy. "I think I want you to come into the office with me. Let's see some ID."

Tynan reached into his hip pocket and pulled out his wallet. He opened it, flipping it around so that the deputy could see his military ID.

"How long you been here?" he asked.

"At this place? Ten minutes. In Arizona? Most of the day."

"Why don't you follow me in?" said the deputy.

"Why?"

"We have a murder investigation in progress and I'd like to talk to you about it."

Tynan shrugged and said, "Aren't you supposed to read me my rights?"

"You're not under arrest. I'd just like you to come in because of a strange coincidence. If you can demonstrate that you arrived in Arizona this morning, then we've got no trouble." He stepped back and put a hand on his pistol.

Tynan grinned because the deputy was within kicking range. He could kill the deputy before he could draw his pistol. But then, there was no reason to do it.

"We'll follow you," said Tynan.

"Good," said the deputy. He walked back to the jeep and then wrote down the license number. "Just follow me," he called.

"More delay," said King.

"But we might learn something," said Tynan. He didn't tell her that a murder in this area bothered him greatly. It could mean that someone had already found the treasure and was protecting it. It could be a coincidence, but he didn't believe in them. It was healthier that way.

8

Even though he'd stood in the shower for twenty minutes, and he had scrubbed his body until it was raw, and even though he'd used a scented soap stolen from his wife's vanity, he could still smell the odor of death. He'd been too close to the bodies. He'd carried them, and now the stench from them was in his clothes and on his body.

After twenty minutes, his wife was at the door, knocking on it gently at first, but when he didn't answer, she hit it harder. "Lloyd, are you all right? What's going on in there?"

Jefferies turned off the water and stood there, dripping. He listened to the hammering at the door and finally yelled out, "What the hell you want?"

"You okay in there?"

"I drowned, what the hell you think?"

"You've been in there for a long time," said the woman.

"What? You monitoring the water use in the house now? You work for the water department or something?" yelled Jefferies. He stepped out of the shower and grabbed a towel, rubbing himself down.

When he was dry, he was still convinced he could smell

77

death on him. He looked into the shower, but didn't want his wife standing at the door yelling at him again. He used her talcum and when that didn't help, splashed on the aftershave she'd given him at Christmas the year before. Finally, he was sure that he had masked the odor.

He left the bathroom, walked to the bedroom and dressed in clean clothes. He sat down on the bed and pulled on a clean pair of socks.

His wife appeared in the doorway and asked, "What's going on?"

"Nothing's going on."

"You never shower in the middle of the day." She leaned against the door jamb, her arms folded. She wore a day dress of a light, flowered material. The top was pinned together. Once she had been a handsome woman, but the years had been unkind to her. Her brown hair was full of gray and her face was wrinkled so that she looked fifty instead of thirty-five. She'd married young, bore seven children but only four survived. There had never been enough money.

"I was hot," he snapped.

"Where are you going now?"

"I got to meet with a couple of people. We've got some business to discuss."

"What kind of business?"

Jefferies stood and moved to the dresser. He plucked his wallet, keys, change and knife from the top, putting all those things into his pockets.

"We got a deal working that might make us some real dough finally."

For an instant she was going to protest. But she'd said things in the past and it had done no good. He'd still gone to his meetings, but he'd gone angry with her. Now it didn't seem worth the effort to fight about it.

"I'll have dinner ready about six," she said.

"Well, I might not be here for dinner," he said. "Couple of things that got to be done."

Without another word, she turned, retreating to the kitchen where she understood what was going on. A small world that belonged to her and her alone. No stress there. Just the quiet hum of the refrigerator. A sink that always had running water and a stove that was fairly new and worked for her. She could lose herself in that world and not have to deal with anything on the outside.

Jefferies stopped at the door of the kitchen and watched as she worked there. "I'll try to make it back for dinner," he said. "The meeting might go a little long."

She couldn't help herself. She turned to face him and asked, "What kind of business do you have late on a Saturday afternoon?"

"Just business. If it works out, you'll be very surprised." Then not wanting to talk about it anymore, he turned and headed for the front door.

He made the trip to the bar in record time, but was still the last to arrive. As he entered, he saw both Boyle and Winters sitting in the rear booth. He walked over to them and slipped in with them.

"Christ," said Winters, "you smell."

Jefferies was suddenly afraid that the odor of the bodies was still on him. "What?" he asked, confused.

"You fall into a vat of Brut or something?"

Boyle laughed. "Yeah. Fall into a vat of Brut."

Jefferies turned, saw the weary waitress and waved at her. "Bring me a Coors." He looked at Winters and said, "I took a shower for Christ sake."

"Fine." He leaned forward and lowered his voice. "Now, I think it's time that we hired some people to help us."

"No," said Jefferies. "I don't want to share the money with any more people."

"I'm not talking about shares," said Winters. "I'm talking about hiring some people to work for us. You've got to get your mind set here. We're not poor. We're rich." He glanced at Boyle and then back at Jefferies. "Very rich, so stop thinking like a poor man."

The waitress brought the Coors, left it and retreated. She didn't bother collecting for it because she knew them all. They wouldn't stiff her for the beer. If they left without paying, they'd pick it up the next time anyway.

"So, what are you saying?"

Winters scratched his chin and said, "We hire ten, twelve guys, at ten thousand a piece, to help us guard the gold. We give each of them a bar of silver as an advance, but tell them not to sell it around here. Take it over to New Mexico or up to Phoenix and find a dealer. Then we've got the manpower to keep people out of the cave."

"Except they'll know," said Jefferies.

"Christ," said Winters. "You take stupid pills or something? We put them in the general area and tell them to keep everyone else out. We don't put them in the cave and if they search for it, we don't care because they won't find it."

"What's that gain us?" asked Jefferies, drinking from the bottle.

"That keeps everyone else away from our gold until I can get the arrangements made in Mexico. Then we get it out of there and take it to Mexico and get the money."

"You have some people in mind for all this?" asked Jefferies. "Some people we can trust?"

"Let me make the arrangements," said Winters. "I'll get them out there to protect our gold." He looked around and added, "You've now got to think like an executive. We have the money not to get our hands dirty. And using only a million dollars, paying the men ten thousand a piece, we can hire a hundred good men and keep them happy for a year."

Boyle interrupted then for the first time. "That's more than we need."

"But it'll keep everyone away from our gold and leave us with a shit pot full for ourselves."

"But what about now? Tonight?" asked Jefferies.

"Christ," snapped Winters. "Do I have to think of everything? We hire a couple of guys for tonight. A hundred dollars a piece. Get them out there now. Then tomorrow, or Tuesday, we can get someone out there on a permanent basis. A hundred dollars isn't going to break us. Not now anyway."

"But they'll know about the gold," said Boyle.

"We don't have to tell them a thing about the gold," said Winters, losing his patience. "We just give them the money to keep people away from the cave. They don't have to know about it or what's in it."

"When do we do this?" asked Jefferies.

"Tonight," said Winters.

It hadn't taken them long to get everything straightened out at the sheriff's office. Tynan had flashed his ID and given them another number to call. It proved that neither of them had been in Arizona before that morning and neither could have been involved in the murders, if they had been committed. Travis still was not convinced that anyone had been killed.

"Then why drag us in here?" Tynan had asked.

"Because I'd look plenty stupid if a murder had been committed and I had let the perpetrators go because I was having trouble establishing the crime. Especially after someone had told me about it. This way everyone is happy."

"I'm not," King had told him. "You took me away from some very important work."

Travis had leaned back, put his feet up on his desk and asked, "What work would that be, Doctor?"

King blushed and then pulled out a cover story. "I'm searching for archaeological evidence that Spanish conquistadors did reach this far north, and did establish a semi-permanent settlement. I'm looking for evidence of the exploitation of the environment and the local natives."

"And you thought you'd find it out there, in the desert away from everything?"

King shrugged. "We were just getting the feel of the area. Driving around and looking over the landscape."

Travis shifted around and dropped his feet to the floor with a quiet thud. "Okay, I'm satisfied with you two. Stick around for a few days."

Tynan looked at him and asked, "Why? We've shown that we're not connected to any crimes in the area. We just got here today, so why should we stick around, if we are suddenly inclined to leave?"

"We have an investigation going," said Travis.

"Not my concern," said Tynan.

Travis nodded and then said, "Let me put it this way. You going to be around for the next couple of days? On your own? With no suggestions from me?"

"Certainly," said Tynan, grinning. "Doctor King has work to do."

"Fine. Thank you for your cooperation."

Tynan and King left the sheriff's office. As they came out the door, two people approached them. The man held out his hand and said, "I'm Jason Collins. Stationed out at the fort. This is Sergeant Sheila Davis. Works out there with us."

Tynan introduced himself and then King followed suit.

"We thought," said Collins, "that if you have nothing else to do, you'd have dinner with us."

"Why?" asked Tynan.

"Well, we were responsible for your being picked up by the sheriff. Not that we meant any harm, but we saw two bodies out there and that's why the sheriff was there."

Tynan wiped a hand over his face. "Just what did you see?" He glanced at King, but she didn't seem interested in the discussion.

"Two people, both of them shot. Looked like a large caliber weapon. We took the deputy out to where it happened but the bodies were gone."

"You sure that you saw two dead people?"

"Don't you start in on us," said Collins. "I was close enough to touch them if I had wanted. They had been shot. They were dead. When we got back out there, the bodies and all evidence of it was gone."

Tynan looked at King and said, "Well, we'll let you buy us a dinner. Tonight. In Bisbee." He gave them the name of the motel and suggested they meet at seven.

They shook hands and then Tynan, along with King, started off toward the parking lot.

As soon as they were out of earshot, she demanded, "Why did you agree to having dinner with them?"

"Because, if their story is true, we could be in trouble. There is no reason for two people to be shot in that section of the desert."

"Unless," interrupted King, "they were getting close to the entrance of the cave."

"The thought had crossed my mind. Besides, we can learn what Collins and Davis were doing out there. These are the preliminaries that we were talking about earlier."

"Okay," she said. "Given what's happened, maybe it's best to go a little slower."

"Can't hurt."

Collins watched the two new people walk away and then looked at Davis. Her color had improved, but she hadn't said much in the last few hours. She'd let others make the decisions and let others tell her what she was going to do.

"We never got to eat," she said finally.

"You want to eat now?"

"No," she said. "It's too bad. I spent a lot of money on that picnic basket. Had it all planned out. Now the day is ruined."

Collins faced her and grinned. "Tell you what. Let's go over to your apartment and see what we can salvage. You'll need to change for dinner."

"That's another thing," said Davis. "Why did you want to have dinner with those people?"

Collins started toward the parking lot to get his car. "I did that because I think it's mighty strange that they showed up when they did."

"You mean they might have had something to do with the murders?"

Collins shrugged. "I don't know. I just think it's strange that they showed up when they did. I don't care what the deputy said. Hell, he didn't even believe us, so it makes sense that he'd let them go."

"So we're doing a little investigating on our own."

They reached the car. Collins unlocked his door and opened it but didn't get inside. The sun had had most of the day to bake the interior and he wanted to give it a chance to cool off before he got in.

Over to the top of his car he said, "What would they be doing out in that very hunk of desert?"

Davis stood there and shrugged. "I don't know."

"Then what were you doing out there?"

"Looking for treasure." She hesitated. "You don't mean that they were out there for the same reason, do you?"

Collins ducked down, leaned across the front seat and opened the other door. He stood up again and said, "That's the only thing that makes sense to me. Suddenly, we've got all kinds of people interested in one section of the desert and the only reason for it would be that gold."

Davis sat down and then stood up again. It was still too hot to sit in the car. To Collins, she said, "So we're going to pump them and find out if they know something."

"Naturally. That treasure has brought hunters into the area for years. That's the only thing that makes sense. If the treasure exists, that's where it has to be."

Again Davis sat down. This time she stayed in the car. Collins joined her and started the engine, turning the air conditioning up to high, letting it blow in. Finally he closed his door and backed out.

"You think they know something about the treasure?" she asked.

"I've been stationed here for almost two years. I've told you that I looked into this thing once or twice and my conclusions, based on my research, is that the treasure is out there somewhere if it's out there at all. They seem to think the same thing."

Davis slid closer to him and touched his arm. "I had such plans for today."

"Yeah," said Collins. He glanced at her. "I know what you mean. But things got turned upside down."

"The treasure isn't that important. It's kind of like running up to Las Vegas and figuring you're going to hit it big on the slot machines. The odds are against you, but what the hell, some people have lucked into it."

Without thinking about it, Collins put his arm around her, gently pulling her closer. She shifted around, leaning against him. The day, the murders, and everything else had driven the thoughts of trouble with the military from his mind. At the moment she was a desirable woman and not an Army NCO. If she had been assigned to another office, he wouldn't have thought twice about dating her.

"I wish we'd had the chance to eat the picnic lunch," said Davis. "I was promised that it was very good."

"You mean you didn't fix it yourself?"

She shrugged. "I wanted it to be just right. I had it made in the deli at the post. They promised everything would be just right and if it wasn't, then I could get my money back by returning the basket."

"Christ, Sheila, I wished you hadn't spent your money on that. I'd have been happy with hamburgers and baked beans."

"I know," she said, but she was feeling good because it was the first time that he'd used her first name since he'd picked her up that morning. It meant that the day might not have been going according to the plan, but progress was being made.

"Anyway," she said, "you can buy my dinner and that'll make up for it. We can always have another picnic tomorrow."

"I suppose we could," said Collins, not realizing what he was committing himself to.

9

Boyle stayed at the bar, sucking down beer and trying not to remember what the bodies lying in the desert had looked like. Winters and Jefferies left, driving to the outskirts of town where they knew they'd find Thomas Mathews, a friend who worked construction when the work was available and who drank beer when it wasn't.

Mathews was sitting outside his trailer, his feet up on the lip of a fifty-five gallon drum that had been cut in half, drinking beer and listening to the ball game on the radio. His dog, tied to a dying tree, barked at them as they stopped the car.

"Shut up, Shithead," yelled Mathews at the barking dog. He threw an empty beer can at the damned mutt when it didn't listen to him.

Winters got out of the car and moved forward. He stopped short and looked down at Mathews. He was a big man with a huge stomach and a beard that covered most of his face. A black curling mass that climbed his cheeks so that only his bright eyes showed. He had shoulder length hair that hadn't been washed recently and that was tied back with a leather cord.

The yard of the trailer was as big a mess as the owner. It was hard packed dirt with no sign of grass. A broken down pick up sat on cinderblocks to the side. The engine was missing as were the seats and the steering wheel.

There was a trash pile that held wooden crates, broken cinder blocks, bottles, papers and magazines. Bottles, empty food cartons, beer cans and newspapers were scattered around the rest of the yard. There was a single, rusting I-beam about four feet long right in front of the door. It might have been an attempt at building a step up.

"What you want, Nate?" asked Mathews. It came out, "Wha' chew wan', Nate?"

"You doing anything?"

"Sitting here listening to the game. I'm doing that right now."

"I mean you got work?"

Mathews shifted around and then shrugged. "Not at the moment, no."

"You wanting some?"

"Always can use some work if the pay's right and the hours ain't too long."

Jefferies came around the other side of the car. "Afternoon, Tom."

"Afternoon, Lloyd."

Winters rubbed his face and then wiped the sweat on his shirt. "Got a hundred dollars for you if you'll spend some time in the desert. Got a hundred dollars for any one you think you're going to need."

Mathews tilted the beer to his lips and drank. "Why're you paying me a hundred for anything?"

"Not me, Tom. A friend. Wants to keep everyone out of his section of the desert. Wants them to stay clear out of his section of the desert and will pay you and a couple of others to make sure they stay out."

Mathews sat up and leaned his elbows on his knees. "Just how far are we supposed to go? How badly does he want to keep people out?"

Winters understood the question and grinned. "You still got that old deer rifle?"

"Yeah."

"Our friend thinks it would be a real good idea if you took it along. You scare them off. They don't scare, then it's up to you to change their minds."

Jefferies was standing in the back, leaning against the front of his car. "We, he, doesn't want anyone walking about out there for a couple of weeks."

"I understand," said Mathews. "How many friends should I take out there?"

Winters looked back at Jefferies and then turned to face Mathews. "I would think that two people tonight and two tomorrow would be just fine."

"A hundred dollars a day?" said Mathews.

"Yeah," said Winters. "We'll talk to you tomorrow if you need to stay longer."

"When do I get paid?"

Winters pulled out his wallet and took out five twenties. He handed them over, counting them out slowly. "Tomorrow, I'll pay the others."

"I'll make a few calls," said Mathews. "Now, where do you want us?"

"You line up the men and then we'll drive you out and show you what we want guarded."

"Fine," said Mathews, standing. "What is it? A speed lab?"

"Nevermind," said Winters. "You just guard the ground and keep everyone out of the area and you'll make some easy dough for yourself."

Mathews disappeared into the trailer. When he was

gone, Jefferies moved closer to Winters and whispered. "That was great. He thinks we're running drugs."

"Doesn't matter what he thinks," said Winters, "as long as he does the job."

Collins sat on the couch, where he'd sat earlier that day, and tried to get himself worked up about the situation. He shouldn't be in Davis's apartment. He should be in his own apartment so that no one could accuse him of forcing Davis to do something she didn't want to do. He was still a captain and she was still a sergeant.

But he didn't want to go. Besides, it wasn't World War Two where the standards of conduct were different. And the regulation was designed to keep enlisted men and female officers apart. So he sat there and drank a glass of white wine and waited for Davis.

When she appeared, ten minutes later, he nearly dropped his wine. She was wearing only bikini panties of a material so filmy that he could see right through them. Nothing was left to the imagination.

"Just wanted to see if there is anything I can get you before I take my shower," she said.

"Nope," said Collins. "I'm fine." He couldn't help staring at her.

She turned, letting him examine her back, but then stopped and looked over her shoulder. "You know, we shouldn't waste water. Not a lot of it here in the desert. Maybe we should shower together."

"You go ahead," said Collins.

She shrugged but didn't walk away. Instead she turned to face him and slowly rolled her panties down her thighs. She straightened with them at her knees and then wiggled her legs. The garment fell to her ankles.

Collins watched the show and felt himself respond. He

knew that if he stood up, she would know that she was getting to him. Casually, he tried to cross his legs, but found he was doubled over or caught in the material, and couldn't complete the motion. He dropped his foot to the floor.

"You could wash my back," she said. "I promise I won't look at you."

"This is not going the way I planned," said Collins. He spoke because he felt he had to say something.

"Sometimes we just have to take a chance," said Davis. She bent slowly and slipped the panties off her feet. She stood clutching them in her left hand. "The offer is still good."

Collins closed his eyes and then finished his wine. When he opened them, Davis was standing there, smiling, and waiting for him to make his decision.

"You know all the rules and regulations about officers and enlisted troops," said Collins.

"They don't apply here," she said. "You have done nothing to force me. I've made all the moves."

Collins sat quietly for a moment and then put his glass down. He wished that he hadn't responded so quickly to her because there was no easy way to stand up. He turned slightly and got to his feet, pulling at the crotch of his pants until he could stand comfortably.

"You didn't have to do that," she said, moving toward him. She unbuckled his belt and unzipped his fly. "I would have been happy to help you."

They walked down the hall and then turned into her bedroom. She helped him take off his clothes, tossing them on the bed. Once he was naked, she turned to him, wrapped her arms around him and pressed her body against his.

"You don't know how long I've dreamed about this.

Since the first day I walked into the office and saw you."

"I've become a sex object."

"Yeah," she said. "Isn't it fun?"

She tilted her head up and kissed him. She felt him respond to her, felt his heart beat as she clung to him.

Finally he pulled away and said, "We've got to meet those others at seven."

"Then you want to shower now?"

"No," said Collins, "but we'll have to."

She walked away from him, heading toward the bathroom. He watched her and then rushed to join her. "It'll make dinner interesting. Thinking about all the things we can do when we get back here."

"Very interesting," she said.

Tynan was sitting at the table, studying the map when there was a knock at the door. He got it and found Collins and Davis standing there.

"Ready?" asked Collins.

"Sure." Tynan turned and yelled for King. She came out of the bathroom. "Let's go."

They decided that the restaurant at the motel would be fine and walked over to it. They were given a table in the back and once they were seated, with menus in hand, Collins started the discussion.

"You're down here from?"

King told him. Then added, "Doing some archaeological research."

"As you said. Any reason that you happened to be out there in that section of the desert?"

Tynan put down his menu and asked, "Any reason why we shouldn't be in that area?"

He nodded at Davis. "We were out there for two reasons. One was for a picnic lunch. Something to do on a

Saturday. A chance to get out with a friend."

"Uh-huh," said Tynan.

"The second reason," said Collins, "was to look for a treasure supposedly hidden in a lost cave." He shrugged, embarrassed.

Tynan kept a straight face. He tried not to look at King. "A treasure?"

"Yes. Legend has it that the Spanish found a very rich mine around here. They dug out gold, smelted it and then stockpiled it, along with silver bullion from another mine. The Spanish planned to ship it to the coast of Mexico but they never got it there. Indians, probably Apaches, attacked, killed everyone and hid the mine. The gold and silver is still there."

King laughed but the sound was high and strained without mirth. "Spanish gold."

"People around here search for it periodically," said Collins. "It's out there, somewhere."

"You believe that?" asked Tynan.

Now Collins glanced at Davis. "I'm not convinced there is anything to the stories. Rumor has it that the Army already found it and it's now at Fort Knox. The government never said anything because the people would demand a reduction of income taxes, though there was only a hundred million or so hidden."

The waitress appeared then. She took the orders and then moved back toward the kitchen. When she did, Collins asked, "Now, what were the two of you doing out there?"

"Like the Doctor said, we were looking for archaeological evidence."

"The desert is a dangerous place," said Collins. "People get killed out there."

"That sounds like a threat," said Tynan.

"Oh no," said Davis. "That's not what we mean. We found bodies out there. Someone killed two people for no reason."

Tynan nodded. "Killed them for no reason, unless you're right about the gold." King kicked him under the table. He ignored her. "Then you've got a motive. Why did you decide to search in that section of the desert?"

Salads arrived. The waitress stood there for a moment, watching them, and then brought over a silver set of bowls that held three types of dressing. Satisfied that the people were happy, she left again.

"You didn't answer the question," said Tynan.

Collins shrugged and grinned sheepishly. "Like everyone else, I've taken a shot at finding the gold. Figuring that it'd do me no good if I found it on Army land, and believing that if it was there, the Army already had it, I concluded this was the most likely site of the cave."

Tynan looked at King but she didn't say anything. "So you were looking for gold?"

"No," said Collins. "I was actually going on a picnic. Sheila was looking for gold."

"Oh."

"But then we found the bodies and that ended our search."

"What do you think that means?" asked Tynan.

"Who knows?" asked Collins. "There are bands of Mexicans who cross the border to steal cars. Maybe they ran into Mexican car thieves. Maybe the husband of the girl or maybe the wife of the man had them killed. Maybe they were just in the wrong place at the wrong time."

Tynan finished his salad. He pushed the bowl to the side and said, "Let's all be honest here."

"About time," said Collins.

Tynan nodded. He glanced at King and knew that he

was talking out of turn, but when they had left on the trip, he hadn't expected bodies to be found as they drove up. The situation had changed radically. The bodies probably were the result of one of the things that Collins suggested, but there was also the possibility that people had been killed because they had gotten too close to the gold. It meant that someone else had already found it. It was the only explanation that fit the facts. All the other cases would have the bodies left where Collins and Davis had found them. The only reason to risk moving them was if you didn't want others, want the police, searching that area of the desert.

King hesitated and then said, "That's the reason we're here. To find the gold."

"I knew it," said Davis. "I knew it. The gold is out there, isn't it?"

King nodded slowly. "We have found documentation that supports the idea of gold around here. We found some papers in the Spanish archives that tell us that a treasure was left in this area."

"So what are you going to do?" asked Collins.

Tynan, surprised that King would talk at all, answered the question. "We've got to figure this out. We didn't figure that anyone would know where the gold is. Now it seems that it's been found."

"If it's been found," said Davis, "I guess we're all out of luck."

"I suppose," said King. "But maybe they just think it's out there. Then it's up for grabs. Until we learn that someone else has found it, we're going to keep looking."

"You need help?" asked Collins.

King shook her head.

But Tynan said, "I think that we should work together. We have some good maps and you have a knowledge of the local terrain. Maybe we can help each other."

"What kind of split?" asked Davis.

"Hell, we'll all make some dough," said Tynan.

But King said, "I'm not sure how the university will respond to our giving away their assets."

"Consultation fees for the locals," said Tynan.

"Of course," said King. She held out a hand, across the table and added, formally, "Welcome to the project."

"Thanks," said Collins. "I always wanted to be involved in an archaeological expedition."

"Sounds better than a treasure hunt, doesn't it?" said Tynan.

"Much."

10

It was dark when Winters, Jefferies, Mathews and his two friends drove out into the desert. They stayed on the back roads, the guns concealed in the trunk. Jefferies, under orders from Winters, took a number of turns that weren't necessary hoping that the men with them wouldn't realize where they were. Winters kept dropping hints that they were going to guard the approaches to a drug lab and that the men in it wouldn't be happy if they walked up to it.

"A hundred bucks apiece," said Winters again. "All you have to do is watch the desert and if anyone shows, chase them away. Tomorrow we'll be back and decide what do to then."

"When do we get paid?" asked LeRoy Jackson. He was a big, black man who might be described as a carbon copy of Mathews except that he appeared to be stronger.

"Tomorrow," said Winters. "Then, if your services are needed for another day, arrangements will be made then."

"Hundred bucks each," said Hank Richards. He was smaller than the other two but meaner. He always felt that his size put him at a disadvantage, so he developed a bad attitude which he inflicted on everyone around him.

"That's right," said Winters.

Jefferies turned down the final road and then drove along it for a mile or a mile and a half. It was along the road that he'd seen the two people and it was the same road they'd used earlier when they had removed the bodies. This time he drove them up into the hills.

Stopping at the crest of a hill, Winters pointed. "You walk along this ridge for a mile. You'll see two arroyos to the south side. In the third, deeper one, more of a flash flood canyon, you walk along the bottom of it and set up in the entrance to it. Watch the desert to the south. Shouldn't be any trouble from the north."

"What about lunch?" asked Mathews.

"We'll be out about noon, maybe an hour or so later but not much. That shouldn't be a hassle for three big, strong boys, should it?"

"Not for a hundred bucks," said Jackson. "Not if we get the dough tomorrow."

Jefferies got out and opened the trunk. Two of the men got out his rifle. Mathews unzipped a smaller case and pulled out a long barreled revolver. He stuck that in the waistband of his dirty jeans.

Richards leaned over and plucked the case of beer from the trunk. He lifted it up to his shoulder. "This'll keep us happy until tomorrow."

"I don't want anyone getting drunk," said Winters.

"Three of us can't get drunk on one case of beer," said Mathews.

"And I don't want anyone walking out to find more beer. Once you're in place, you stay there until morning, even if you run out of beer. Got it?"

"We got it," said Mathews.

"Remember where to go?"

"We're not retarded," said Mathews.

"Then Lloyd and I'll be back tomorrow with your dough."

Jackson picked up his weapon, a box of rounds and a hunting knife. "Don't be late. I've got a meeting with a friend about six and she's hot to trot."

"We'll be back," said Winters. "You men be careful out there and not go fucking around."

"We can take care of ourselves."

"Right."

Mathews turned and started off along the ridgeline. Jefferies and Winters watched them until they faded in the dark. When they were gone, Jefferies asked, "You think we can trust them?"

"They can handle this. Couple of days we won't need them anymore."

Jefferies turned to walk back to the driver's seat. As he climbed in, he said, "I'll be glad when I'm rich."

"So will I," said Winters.

After dinner, they all returned to Tynan's motel room and examined the maps they had brought. King told them what they had found in the various archives, and Collins added what he had learned from the local legends. Everyone seemed to know the origins of the legend, of the Spanish massacre, but there things changed. Estimates of the value ranged from a hundred million up to half a billion dollars.

The location, however, was a different story. Locally, people believed it was on the Fort Huachuca grounds proper, it was in the Whetstone Mountains, situated in a prominent pass there, it was near Tombstone and was the real reason for the gunfight at the OK Corral, or that it was just across the border in Mexico. There were as many rumors about the location as there were people with an opinion about the treasure.

King told them that all rumors, stories and legends were wrong. It didn't take much to convince Collins and Davis because they'd been out in the area of desert where King thought the treasure was hidden. They'd independently decided on the same location based on different evidence.

They decided to meet the next morning. Collins would bring his rifle, just in case they ran into trouble. Although the sheriff hadn't found the bodies of the murder victims, Collins and Davis seemed too steady to invent such a story. They'd be ready for everything.

After they were gone, with Tynan sitting in one of the chairs and King sitting on the bed, he asked, "How is the university going to react to your giving away part of the treasure?"

"Given the circumstances, I don't think there's much they can say. There's a real possibility that someone else has already found it and therefore it belongs to them."

Tynan loosened his tie and stood up, stretching. "I've a question for you. Almost all land in this country belongs to someone. The land where the cave and mine is located belongs to someone. How were you going to get the treasure out without having to deal with that?"

"Our legal department has come up with a contract. If we find the treasure, we then attempt to obtain permission to operate on the land."

"I don't know that much law, but that seems to border on fraud."

"We've merely dealing with the landowner from a position of power," said King.

"Isn't there a concept of consideration?" asked Tynan.

"There may be," said King. "As I understand it, we end up giving the landowner a ten or twenty percent cut, which could add up to ten or twenty million dollars. Most people would consider that adequate since they didn't have it and didn't know they had it until we had found it."

Tynan moved to the dresser and picked up the ice bucket. "I'm going to get a Coke and some ice. You want one?"

"Sure."

Tynan left the room and walked out into the late evening heat. He had always thought the desert got cold at night because the sand didn't hold the heat, but that didn't seem to be true here. Even with the sun gone, it was hot out. The short walk to the Coke and ice machine covered him with sweat.

As he stood there, he thought about this whole treasure hunting venture. King seemed honest enough. She was just going along with the others at the university. Scout the situation and see what they could find. But then they had taken it a step farther. They had plans for obtaining signatures after the treasure was located. Ten million dollars was a lot of money to allow someone to search for treasure on your land, unless it was stacked next to a hundred million. Or two hundred million. Or whatever the gold was worth on today's market.

He got the Cokes and the ice and returned to the room. He opened the door and slipped in. The television was on but turned way down. It was more like a dim light than anything else. He set the Cokes on the table and then spotted King. She had removed her clothes and climbed into bed. The air conditioner was humming under the window, kicking out a stream of cold air, keeping it comfortable in the room.

"I take it the discussion is over," said Tynan.

"Pour me some of that Coke," she said, pointing. She sat

up so that the covers fell away, revealing her body in the dim light of the television screen.

Tynan did as asked and handed her a glass. She took a sip and then said, "What did you want to discuss?"

"I don't know. It just seems you're not playing fair with all the people involved in this. The landowner is going to get screwed."

"Listen," she said, "it's not quite as cut and dried as you think. The landowner might end up with nothing at all. There are tax questions that we haven't even addressed. There are many interpretations to the tax law that need to be ironed out. Is it straight income, a capital gain or a windfall? What tax rate applies? Could the IRS legally take upwards of ninety percent of the money?"

"Hadn't thought of that," said Tynan.

"And there are various federal laws that might prevent the landowner or us from keeping any of the money. The Department of the Interior could gain sovereign prerogative and if that doesn't work there is a law drafted in 1906 that was designed to deal with Civil War relics that has been applied to other antiquities. So as you can see there is no guarantee that we, as the finders, or that the landowners where it is found, will retain any of the money."

Tynan shook his head and filled a second glass with Coke. "Then what are you doing here?"

"Well, even if the government snatches it all away from us, the publicity would help the university . . ."

"I thought they wanted to keep their treasure hunting activities under wraps."

"Only if we fail," she said. "A success the first time out will just prove that we'd thought this through carefully. There would be no ridicule then. All the others would be irritated that they hadn't thought of it first."

Tynan moved to the bed and sat down. "Where does this leave the landowner?"

"In the worst case, the landowner is screwed completely. The treasure would be removed from his land, the IRS would be there with a hand out for a piece of the treasure he doesn't legally own, anyone hurt in removing the treasure could sue him, the landowner, and the government would have no obligation to return the land to its original state after the treasure was removed by them."

"Then why do this?" asked Tynan.

"Because it's there. Because we can. Because even if we lose all the money, we could learn so much from the way the mine was constructed, the materials used in it, any tools or artifacts that we find. The treasure extends beyond gold and silver, and the knowledge is something the IRS wouldn't care about."

Tynan set his glass on the nightstand and turned to her. "I knew it wasn't greed that was motivating you."

"You should have known that because there is no way that I'll get any of the treasure except in the form of a higher salary, if the university is lucky enough to retain any of the loot."

Tynan kicked off his shoes and leaned back, against the headboard of the bed. He turned so that he could look at King. The sheet was down to her waist and she had one bare leg outside the covers. Suddenly he wasn't all that interested in the treasure and the legal problems that could be found along with it.

Holding the Coke glass against her chest, both hands on it, and looking toward the TV screen, she said, "I'm bothered by those murders."

Tynan understood what she was saying. "It would seem that your claim to the treasure would be the second, if the murders were committed to keep the victims away from the cave or mine entrance."

"Or third if you count the landowner," she said. "Though I think the law would prevent anyone who had committed a murder from profiting, especially if the gold was on land that belonged to someone else."

Tynan reached over and picked up his Coke. He drank, finishing it, and returned it to the nightstand. "This is more complicated than I thought. You can't just go wandering around, stumble over a treasure trove and be set for the rest of your life."

"Does kind of take the romance out of it, doesn't it? If gold wasn't so heavy, then you'd be able to get in and get out with it. If we were talking about jewels, diamonds or rubies or emeralds, you could carry a couple million dollars in one pocket."

"No jewels in this one though?"

King shook her head. "The list we found told of gold bars and silver bars and that's it. Any precious stones would have had to have been imported from somewhere else and there was no motivation to do that."

Tynan slipped down and laced his fingers behind his head. Staring up at the ceiling, he said, "This has not been the trip I thought it would be. I thought of something along the lines of the search for King Solomon's Mines. Tramping through jungle or across desert. I didn't expect to drive up and be met by the police checking out a murder. This is just no fun."

King set her Coke glass to the side, rolled over and put her head on his shoulder. He could see her bare back and the rise of her bottom. He rubbed her shoulders.

"At least I'm here," she said.

"And I'm getting to see a part of Arizona I've never been to," added Tynan.

She reached up and pulled off his tie. She began unbuttoning his shirt slowly, kissing his bare chest as she exposed it. "I'll do my best to make the trip more fun for you." She fumbled with his belt, finally getting it open.

"Anything you can do will be greatly appreciated."

"I know."

11

Both Tynan and King were ready when there was a knock on the door. Tynan opened it and let Collins and Davis in. They were dressed for a day in the desert. Long sleeve shirts and pants, boots and hats. They wanted to keep the exposed skin to a minimum, especially after the sunburns they had acquired the day before. The situation had changed from the day before when they were just out for a couple of hours.

"Either of you want a Coke?" asked Tynan.

"For breakfast?" said Collins.

"Why not? I prefer something cold and orange juice just doesn't have much caffine in it."

"You ready to go?" asked Davis.

"Set," said Tynan. "But let's check the maps one last time to make sure that we're on the same wavelength."

King came out of the bathroom and said, "Good morning. Everyone ready?"

"We want one last look at the maps," said Tynan.

They all crowded around the table and studied them. King said, "I've been thinking about this and there is no reason for us to walk across the desert here. There must be a road that gets us up into these hills here. That would be the best place to begin the search."

"You mean along the arroyos here?"

"No, over a little bit," she said. "I remembered some-one talking about a pass through the hills. That would be this area. Somewhere along here."

"I think there's a road no more than a mile from that. We can walk along a ridgeline and then down to the floor of the arroyo."

"That's where we'll start then," said King.

"What about breakfast?" asked Tynan.

Davis said, "I packed some sandwiches in case we got hungry. Let's just get going. We keep screwing around and never get out there to look."

"Then let's go," said King. "I'm not hungry."

Tynan walked over to his suitcase, opened it and took out his Browning M-35. With his back to them so that he was concealing his motions, he slapped a magazine home, chambered a round and then eased the hammer down. Turning, he slipped the pistol into the waistband of his pants so that it was seated in the small of his back. Not the most comfortable way to carry it, but a hasty search some-times would miss it.

As he turned, no one said a word about the pistol. They pretended that he didn't have it. All of them were thinking of the two bodies found out there that the sheriff refused to admit existed. If there was no crime, there was no case and his records were clean.

They left the room with King locking the door behind them. She had gathered up her maps and the few docu-ments that related to the treasure, figuring that anyone searching the room would find nothing to suggest they were interested in the Huachuca horde.

Outside, Collins moved his hunting rifle from the back

seat to the floor. He pointed at the jeep and said, "We can travel cross country in this if we have to. Borrowed it from a friend for the day."

"Good move," said Tynan.

Collins took the driver's seat. Tynan and King climbed in the back and Davis rode shotgun. They drove out, into the early morning mists, turned north on the highway, and headed out of Bisbee. It wasn't long before they turned off the main highway, took Highway 90 toward Sierra Vista and then began traveling a series of dirt and gravel roads. One of them was nothing more than a track across part of the desert, but it joined with a gravel road.

They slowed and King monitored their progress on one of the maps they had brought. Tynan used a compass and they searched for the obvious landmarks.

"We're getting close," she said.

Collins nodded and said, "I hadn't noticed it before, but the place where we found the bodies would be to the west of here. Maybe a mile. Maybe less."

Tynan pointed to the north. "Then we want to climb up into those hills and stop near the crest."

King, still watching the map, glanced up, then down, and confirmed what Tynan had said. "Looks right to me."

At the top of the hill, Collins pulled to the side of the road and turned off the engine. Stretched out in front of them was a low valley. Haze lingered in it, but it could have been dust rather than a mist. There seemed to be a dry lake bed that looked as if someone had bulldozed it to level it at some point. Then, much farther was another set of hills. They too could mask the site of the cave entrance.

Sitting there all four of them realized just how large the task in front of them was going to be. Each knew that beyond the far hills was another set of them and then another. To the south were hills and to the east were hills.

There were passes through each of them. A thousand places where the lost mine could be hidden.

King folded her map and said, "Maybe this isn't such a great idea. Sitting in a room looking at the map doesn't give you the feel for the vastness of the spaces."

Tynan shielded his eyes with a hand and said, "If I was to guess, I'd guess that we're close right here."

"Why? Because of those murders?" asked Davis.

"No," said Tynan. "Because the bodies disappeared. That's the one thing that bothers me. It means that whoever did it had a reason for moving them and the only thing that makes sense to me was that he didn't want to have the police searching in this area."

Collins climbed out of the jeep. He stood facing the ridgeline and then glanced over his shoulder. "Let's get going then."

Davis got out and Tynan tilted the seat up, out of the way. He bent over and retrieved the rifle, handing it to Collins. Then, carefully, he got out. King followed him. They passed out the equipment then. Tynan held onto the compass and each of them took a canteen. Collins had a snakebite kit and a hunting knife. King had her maps. Tynan left his pistol concealed. He hung binoculars around his neck.

"I guess that's everything," said Tynan.

Collins checked his watch. "Outbound for no more than four hours. Then we'll have to head back. No farther. When the time's up we head back."

"Agreed," said Tynan. He glanced at King.

"I think we follow this ridgeline past two arroyos and then down into the third. The legend seems to suggest that you can see the southern side of the pass from the cave mouth, so we'll turn in that direction but it could be a mile or more from the entrance to the end of the pass."

"Okay," said Tynan, adjusting the pistol belt that held his canteen and first aid kit. "Let's do it."

"I'll lead," said King.

Tynan watched as she stepped down from the hard surface of the road, walked up to the ridgeline and began to move along it. As he joined her, he couldn't help but feel a pulsing excitement bubble through him. When all was said and done, they were looking for a treasure. A real treasure filled with mystery and legend. Just like the men and women in search of King Solomon's Mines. Even with the IRS and the Department of the Interior lurking somewhere in the background, he was excited about finding the gold. Even if all he got to do was look at it before surrendering it to the government.

Mathews sat with his back against a boulder, nestled in a crevice that protected him from the morning sun and concealed him from those who might be crossing the open desert in front of him. Jackson was asleep in the shade, his head cradled on his arm. Richards sat sixty feet to the right, near the floor of the arroyo where he could see out, to the east. That part of the desert was blocked from Mathews's view by the lay of the land.

He picked up a beer can, shook it and then tilted it up to his lips. There was a thin trickle of luke warm liquid. If they'd been smart, they'd have brought another case of beer.

He glanced down at Jackson and then slid down to him and kicked him in the foot. Jackson sat up suddenly, blinked in the brightening of the morning and asked, "What the fuck?"

"You was snoring."

"Not," said Jackson.

"Doesn't matter," said Mathews. "Your turn for the

watch so that I can catch a little shut eye before it gets too hot to sleep."

Jackson stretched, his arms over his head. "You see anything?"

"Nothing moving anywhere."

"What about shithead?"

"Leave him where he is. Do him good. Besides he's getting a hundred bucks just like us so why worry about him?"

"Any beer left?"

"Nope. Finished the last of it about dawn," said Mathews. "Got some water."

Jackson stood up and looked out over the desert. "Anything moving out there?"

"Nothing." Mathews sat quietly then, staring out. "Nothing at all."

Jackson moved over to him and crouched near the empty beer cans. He picked them up one at a time and tossed them away as he discovered that there was nothing in them.

"Getting hungry," said Jackson.

"Nothing we can do about that."

Jackson took the rifle and then sat down with his back to the boulder. He slowly scanned the horizon, saw no one out there and then asked, "You know what's going on?"

"Winters came to get me and offered the money. That's all I know. I figure it's worth it for the money and I don't care what we're protecting." He lay down where Jackson had been.

Jackson kicked the case that held the empty beer cans. "Maybe we should send Richards out for something to drink."

"No," said Mathews. "We'll just have to suffer through

the morning." He rolled to his back and put an arm over his eyes. "Wake me in a couple of hours."

"Sure."

King stopped once after thirty minutes and checked her map again. She pointed down one of the arroyos and said, "This has got to be the place."

Tynan lifted his binoculars to his eyes and examined the terrain. It was completely barren. There was no sign that anyone had ever walked in the arroyo. There was no trash in it and no roads or trails. There was nothing that looked as if it concealed the entrance to a cave or a mine. He had suspected that there would have been a dump near the mine, a place where the material that had been dug from it had been dumped. It would give a clue about the mine. But there was no evidence that anyone had worked in that arroyo.

When Tynan finished, King started down, off the ridgeline. The sand was loose and they used the rocks and boulders to climb down. The floor of the arroyo was almost as solid as concrete. It was a flat floor covered with the rubble of broken rock. The cuts and folds in the hills concealed smaller valleys. There were areas protected by rocks, arches and holes that would keep out the rain, if it ever rained.

"Give me half a dozen men and I could keep a battalion pinned down for a month," said Collins.

Tynan sat down on a rock and pulled out his canteen. He took a deep drink and put the canteen away. He rubbed his face and then wiped the sweat on his shirt.

"This is going to be an impossible task unless we can think of a way to speed the process. Take us a week to search the area in front of us and if the Spanish tried to hide it, we might walk right by it."

"Spanish didn't hide it, the Apaches did," said King.

"Doesn't matter who it was. The point is that someone tried to conceal the entrance."

King sat down on the ground. She scooped up a handful of the gray sand and let it dribble through her fingers. It produced a fine dust. The same kind of dust that seemed to cover everything in the arroyo. She then dusted her palms together.

"So you have an idea?" asked King.

"That's just it," said Tynan, "I don't. If the mine had been worked recently, sometime in the last hundred years or so, we might be able to find the slag pile, but that would have eroded away by now."

"Let's think this through," said Collins. "There must be some clues to the entrance."

Tynan shook his head. "Not if no one has been in it for three or four hundred years. If the Apaches filled in the entrance to hide it, there would be no evidence of that. We'd have to know where to dig to find it."

"Damn," said King. "We've got to be close."

"Didn't any of those records you read give you any clues?" asked Davis.

King looked at the other woman. "Nothing that appears on a modern map. There is a reference to a village called San Sebastian de Lopez, but we could find nothing that relates to it. It's probably a village established by the Jesuits that was abandoned after the massacre and disappeared in the intervening centuries."

Tynan leaned forward, elbows on his knees. "A metal detector won't help."

"Why not?" asked Collins. "We're talking about a large pile of metal. Even if it's buried ten, twelve, fifteen feet down, a good metal detector would pick it up."

"We should have thought of that before," said King.

"Not really," said Tynan. "We need to see the terrain first. That way we know what we need."

"The legend claims that the cave faces the mouth of a pass through the hills. That would be south of here. Maybe things will change. Maybe we'll see some of those clues down there," said King.

Collins checked his watch. "We've a couple of hours if we want to use them."

"We're here," said Davis. "Let's look around. I didn't get a chance yesterday."

Tynan stood up. He said, "I think we need to stick close to the sides of the arroyo. You two over there and King and me over here. That'll give us a better look at the sides."

"Let's go," said Davis. She was having trouble standing still.

Collins started off to the western side of the arroyo, walking at the foot of the slope. He was studying it as he moved. Davis was right behind him.

"You ready?" Tynan asked King.

"Sure."

They started off. Tynan stopped periodically and used his binoculars to examine the sides of the arroyo. There were shadows that suggested something hiding in the folds of the land, but as he moved, he saw that they were no more than just depressions and furrows in the land. Nothing that could hide a cave entrance.

They kept at it for about an hour, walking along in the hot, desert sun. Sweat dripped, soaking their clothes, and they drank their water quickly. They moved slowly, trying to conserve their strength as the heat built. Sunlight reflected from the gray sand so that it looked almost as if it was sun on snow. And there was a shimmering in the distance. Heat rising from the sand.

The shot caught them by surprise.

Tynan dived to the right and rolled over behind a rock. King was only a second slower. She knew exactly what had happened, but didn't move immediately. Then she jumped, landing behind a boulder. Collins hit the ground, his rifle up, trying to spot the enemy, whoever it was.

Only Davis failed to react. She stood there, saw the dirt kicked up and heard the sound of the shot. Then she screamed once and turned to run.

There was a second shot, this one whining off a rock. Collins was then up, running to his right. He climbed part of the way up the slope, sliding in the soft sand. He tried to run, his feet slipping, throwing up sand. He jumped forward and dropped down behind a rock.

Davis continued to run. She dodged left and then right. The third round hit a rock and a piece of flying stone hit her cheek. She reached up, felt the wetness on her face and then fell. An instant later she scrambled to her feet and ran blindly up the arroyo, all thoughts of treasure forgotten. All she could see were the bodies of the dead man and the dead woman, bullet holes in them.

"Help me!" she said. "Someone help me."

12

Richards saw them first. He had a better angle on it and had turned his attention across the arroyo to where Mathews and Jackson were hiding when he caught the movement out of the corner of his eye. He turned to see two people walking along the base of the slope, looking up at it as if searching for something. Remembering what he had been told as they had been brought out there, he didn't hesitate. He raised his rifle and snapped off a shot.

The first shot was wild. It hit the ground in the center of the arroyo. One of the men dived for cover. Two of the others were a second slower but they were gone by the time he managed to work the bolt of his hunting rifle. The last of them had turned and was running away.

He fired again. He heard the bullet ricochet and saw the fleeing figure fall. But then she was up and running again and nearly out of sight then. He cranked off the last round and then that person was gone too.

"What the hell you shooting at?" called Mathews. He was standing up, on the other side of the arroyo, his hands to his mouth.

"People," yelled Richards. He didn't stand, afraid that someone would shoot back at him.

"Where?"

"Back there a couple of hundred yards. Three or four of them."

Mathews dropped to the ground and scrambled around. His head poked up from behind the rocks. He searched and then disappeared. Richards worked the bolt of his rifle and then tried to find a new target. He didn't use the scope mounted on his weapon because the field of vision was too small to make it useful.

He caught some movement and swung his rifle around. He saw a flash of cloth and pulled the trigger. Through the scope, he saw the round strike the ground in front of a stone, throwing up a cloud of dust.

"Let's go get them," yelled Mathews.

Richards worked the bolt of the rifle and then stood up. He kept his eyes on the ground in front of him. He felt his heart pounding in his chest and he was covered with sweat. He ducked his head, using his shoulder to wipe away the perspiration. Then, clutching his rifle in both hands, he started down the slope, slipping and sliding to the arroyo floor.

Across from him, both Mathews and Jackson were up and moving. Jackson held the hunting rifle and Mathews had a pistol in his hand. He raised his other hand to his mouth and shouted, "You better come out."

That was greeted with silence.

All of them reached the floor of the arroyo, Richards hidden in the shadows. He knelt there, searching for the people who had sneaked up behind them.

Mathews slapped Jackson on the shoulder and pointed to a position ten feet up the slope where there was a huge rock. Jackson nodded and sprinted up there, crouching near the boulder, his rifle pointed in the general direction of the unidentified people.

"If you make us come to find you, it's going to be that much rougher. You just come out here now."

Again no one spoke.

"All right," said Mathews his voice loud. "We're coming after you." He took a single step.

There was one shot, the bullet snapped by his head. Mathews stood rooted to the spot, stunned. Jackson fired back, working the bolt of the rifle as fast as he could. The shots echoed in the narrow confines of the arroyo, bouncing off the walls and rock.

Mathews whirled and rushed up the slope. He slipped once, falling to his stomach, and scrambled up, to the boulder where Jackson hid. He shoveled handfuls of dirt out of the way, throwing them to the rear as he tried to pull himself higher. Finally in the shadow of boulder, he fell, his back against the stone. He was breathing heavily.

"That asshole Winters didn't say that these clowns would be armed," gasped Mathews.

Jackson had emptied his rifle and had ducked back. He looked at the other man and said, "What are we supposed to do now? We can't move closer to them without getting our butts shot off by them."

Mathews blinked rapidly and then wiped his face. "They can get out the way they came." He looked at his watch. "But if Winters shows up, he should come from that direction and we'll have them trapped between us."

"If they stay put," said Jackson.

When the firing broke out, Tynan had dived for cover. He had twisted around, behind the rock, searching for the enemy. Reaching up under his shirt to grab his Browning, he rolled right, for the protection of the rocks. Momentarily safe, he checked out the others. King was on the ground behind a pile of rocks, her head cradled in her arms. Collins had scrambled up the other side of the arroyo and knelt behind a rock, his rifle in his hands. He didn't fire back at their attackers. He waited for someone to tell him what to do next.

Davis was running away. He saw her disappear around a bend in the arroyo. There were a couple of shots, but they didn't hit her. She just kept running, screaming for someone to help her. She fell once but was then back on her feet.

"You okay?" whispered Tynan.

King looked at him and nodded. "What in the hell is going on?" she asked.

"I don't know," said Tynan.

"Here they come," called Collins.

From down the arroyo, one of them called out, telling Tynan to give up and that it would go easier on them. Ordering them all to come out. Tynan slipped around, down the hill slightly. He aimed his pistol and pulled the trigger once.

The men turned and fled. They scrambled from sight. One of them started pumping out rounds. He wasn't aiming them, but shooting rapidly, trying to keep everyone pinned down.

Finally the shooting stopped and everyone had disappeared. Tynan kept his eyes searching the front of the arroyo, trying to spot the enemy. He knew where two of them hid, but couldn't see the other. He knew there were at least three of them, even though he'd lost sight of them.

"Collins?"

"Yeah?"

"You okay?"

"I'm fine. You see where they are?"

Tynan decided that he didn't want the shooters to know how much he knew. "No. Keep you're eyes open and shoot at anything that moves out there."

King whispered at him, "You think he'll actually shoot?"

"Doesn't matter," said Tynan. "It'll give those other guys something to think about it. Maybe keep them where they are for right now."

"So what are we going to do?"

Tynan wiped the sweat from his forehead but kept his pistol pointed forward at the enemy. "Right now we stay put. Let them make a move. If we're lucky, they'll just get out."

King shifted around and looked at the arroyo, examining it closely. "I don't understand this."

"Neither do I."

Winters and Jefferies were standing behind the jeep they had found parked on the side of the road. They had checked it out, searching it as best they could. There was nothing in it that told them who it belonged to or why it was parked out there with no one around it.

"Maybe we should just take the license number," said Jefferies.

"And then what? Call the sheriff and ask him to run it for us?"

"So what do we do?" asked Jefferies.

"Wait for the people who own it to come back and talk to them then."

They were walking back to their car when the first shot was fired. Jefferies looked at Winters and then turned toward the west.

"Has to be Mathews and his friends."

"Shooting at the people from the jeep?"

"Has to be," said Winters. "Let's go check it out." He moved to the car and opened the trunk and took out a rifle.

Jefferies did the same and then asked, "We going to kill them?"

"Sounds like we're going to have to."

The shooting increased. Dull pops in the distance. Winters slammed the lid and began to run, trotting to the top of the ridge. Then, remembering some of his military training, he worked his way down the reverse side so that he couldn't be seen from the arroyo. Jefferies was right behind him.

They hurried along, gasping for breath. Running in the loose sand on the side of the slope was like trying to run through thigh high surf with the tide flowing out. Winters stumbled once and put out a hand to steady himself. He slowed then.

As they came closer to the arroyo where Mathews and his friends were hidden, they slowed. Winters held up a hand, waving at Jefferies to stop him. Then, keeping low, Winters worked his way to the top of the ridge. As he got closer, he crouched, and then got down on his stomach, crawling to the top. Just under the summit, he stopped to listen. The firing had stopped.

He continued up, peeking over the top. At first the floor of the arroyo below him was vacant. But then, running toward him was a woman. She didn't seem to have any idea what she was doing or where she was going.

Jefferies, who had joined him, asked, "Do we kill her?"

"No. Let's capture her for now. We can always shoot her later."

"Where's she going?"

Winters didn't answer the question. Instead he pushed Jefferies to the right so that they'd be able to swoop down on her from two directions.

The woman apparently didn't see them. She was lost in the panic of flight. She was running to be running with no thought about where she was going. Following the path of the least resistance.

Winters slipped down from the top of the ridge and then stood. He ran along the slope, on the side away from her, paralleling her path. He tried to get in front of her and came back up to the top of the ridge. He ran over the top, and used the lay of the land and the boulders to conceal himself from her. He reached the arroyo floor and crouched behind a large rock. Opposite him was Jefferies. Winters held his hand up, telling Jefferies to stay where he was.

The woman appeared at the far end of the arroyo, running along, screaming over and over, "Someone help me."

Winters waited for her. He set his rifle down with the butt in the sand and the barrel propped against the rock. He put both hands on the ground, like a sprinter at the starting line. When she came up even with him, he leaped out.

She never saw him. He caught her around the waist in a flying tackle and knocked her to the ground. She screamed once and then Winters fell on her, crushing the wind from her. She wanted to scream but couldn't. She wanted to flee, but couldn't.

Jefferies ran out and stood over the two of them, his pistol pointed at her face. Winters rolled away from her and got to his feet. Davis lay on her side, trying to breathe. As she got her breath back, she sat up and looked up, first at Winters and then at Jefferies and his pistol.

"What's going on?" she demanded.

"I'll ask the questions," said Winters. "Who the hell are you and what are you doing here?"

"Someone was shooting at us."

"That doesn't answer the question," said Winters.

She turned and started to get up. Winters reached down and pushed her back.

"I want to know who you are and what the hell you're doing out here. In this place."

Davis again looked at the pistol pointed at her head. She remembered the face of the woman who had been shot and she began to cry. At first it was a single sob, but that broke the dam. Her shoulders shook and the tears flowed and she wasn't able to talk and was barely able to breathe.

"Let's just kill her," said Jefferies.

"NO!" Winters snapped his fingers and held out a hand. "Give me the gun."

"It's mine," said Jefferies.

"Then put it away and shut up. We're not going to kill anyone." He looked at Davis. "Especially anyone who listens to us and who answers our questions quickly and accurately."

Davis looked up and tried to gain control of her emotions. She wiped her eyes with a hand and sniffed. The sobbing had slowed. She took a deep breath, but refused to look up at either of the men. She kept her eyes on the sand.

"Who are you?" Winters asked again.

"Sheila Davis," she said.

"And what are you doing out here, in the desert? In this part of the desert?"

"A hike," said Davis. "We were out on a hike and somebody started shooting at us. For no reason tried to kill us. Just started shooting at us."

"Good," said Winters. "Very good. Now, how many of you are there and what are your armaments?"

"We didn't have any guns. We were out on a hike and they started shooting at us."

Winters shook his head. "We had been doing so well and now you have to go and lie to us." He turned and walked back to the rock where his rifle waited. Once he had it, he turned. Leaning back on the rock, he said, "How many guns?"

"None. We were on a hike."

"Now why don't I believe that?"

Davis shrugged and started to cry again. "Just let me go. I don't know anything. I won't tell anyone anything. I promise I won't tell."

Winters rubbed his chin and then shook his head. "I can't do that now. You're too value to me. You can help convince your friends to give themselves up."

"They won't listen to me."

Winters looked at Jefferies. "Let's take her to the cave. We can keep her there until we need her."

"That a smart thing to do?"

"Right now it seems to be the only thing to do." He slung his rifle and moved back to where Davis sat, crying quietly. "Up. On your feet."

Slowly she got up. As she did, Jefferies said, "I don't like taking her to the cave. I don't like that at all."

"After a few days there won't be any reason for her not to know where the cave is." He waited for Jefferies to start toward it. Once he did, Winters nodded and Davis fell in behind him with Winters bringing up the rear.

A hundred yards back up the arroyo, Jefferies turned to the west and entered a small side channel. He stopped and looked at Winters who nodded.

Jefferies shrugged and then bent down. He worked his fingers under a flat stone and lifted it, pushing it to the side. He pulled a couple of other rocks away, rolling them to the side. A blast of cool air bubbled out of the dark hole that he had exposed. Leaning forward, he took a lantern out of the darkness and then pumped it up, lighting it.

"Okay, my dear," said Winters. "You may enter."

"Oh no," she said, shaking her head violently. "I don't want to go down there. No."

"Why not?"

"Because. I don't."

Winters shrugged and said, "But that is the reason you're out here. The reason all you are out here and the reason we are out here. Inside that cave is the lost treasure of Fort Huachuca."

Davis stared at him, but the words failed to register. She didn't realize that the man was about to show her the gold that she had wanted to look for. At that moment she didn't care. All she wanted was to get out of there.

"Let's go," said Winters. "Down inside and no one will get hurt."

Jefferies entered the cave then, taking the lantern with him.

"Please," said Winters.

Davis shrugged and followed. Winters was right behind so there was no chance to escape. Down to the lost treasure that so many had tried to find.

13

Tynan shifted around, trying to keep from exposing himself, and yet to get in a better position to see down the arroyo toward the mouth of it he had to move. He glanced over at King who was huddled in the shadow of a boulder, lying on her side with her legs drawn up and her head down, doing her best not to be seen by the riflemen.

"Relax," said Tynan.

She looked at him and tried to smile. Her skin was pale and sweat drenched. Her hair hung down, looking as if she'd just stepped from the shower. She wiped away some of the perspiration with the sleeve of her shirt.

Tynan turned his attention back down the arroyo but the men were still concealed, apparently content to wait. Tynan didn't like that. When someone showed great patience, too often it meant they had an ace in the hole and could afford to wait.

"Okay," he said. "Let's all get out of here. If we retreat back, up the arroyo, we should be able to get clear without exposing ourselves too much."

"What about Sheila?" asked King.

"She ran back the way we came. We should be able to

find her up there. She's probably at the jeep wondering why the rest of us don't get out too."

Tynan turned and looked to the right where Collins was crouched by a boulder. He held his rifle in both hands and was peeking over the top of the rock, searching for the riflemen. Tynan whistled once. A short, loud blast. Collins turned to look at him.

Using hand signals, Tynan told Collins to withdraw. Move to the rear, along the slope of the arroyo and then around the bend. Collins nodded his understanding.

"Okay," said Tynan, "get out now."

King just looked at him.

"Pull straight back, staying low. Use the cover available and once around the bend, take off as fast as you can."

"What are you going to be doing?"

"I'm going to be guarding the rear," said Tynan.

King didn't move immediately but Collins did. Tynan watched as Collins worked his way along the slope of the arroyo. At first he moved slowly, staying low, but as he put some distance between himself and the riflemen, he began to move faster. He came down off the slope, hesitated for a moment, crouching, and then sprinted up the draw, disappearing.

King waited, but no one fired at Collins. She crawled away, mimicking soldiers in war movies, pulling herself along with her hands and pushing with the sides of her feet. She scrambled to the rear, moving her arms and legs like an alligator running across the bank of a river.

She slipped down the slope, sliding in the soft sand. As she reached the floor of the arroyo, she got slowly to her feet. Once she glanced over her shoulder and then leaped up. She ran off, her arms and legs pumping. She turned the corner and disappeared from sight.

With both Collins and King clear, Tynan rolled to his

back and checked his pistol, making sure that he hadn't gotten any sand in it. He'd only fired one shot from it so it was nearly fully loaded. He didn't expect to need any more than the thirteen rounds in it. By shooting, he'd told his enemy that he too was armed. That would slow them down.

He rolled back to his stomach and surveyed the terrain in front of him. No one had moved in the last few minutes. Militarily, the exfiltration was going exactly as planned.

King caught up to Collins just around the bend of the arroyo where he'd stopped to catch his breath and to wait for King and Tynan.

King dropped to the sand as she came around the corner. She was breathing hard.

"Where's Tynan?" he asked.

"Covering us," she said. "Wanted us to get clear before he left his position."

"We're clear now," said Collins.

"You seen Davis?"

Collins shook his head. "She's probably back at the jeep waiting for us."

"That's what Mark said."

Collins continued to watch the arroyo, searching for signs of a pursuit. He glanced at King and said, "I suppose that we could pull back farther. To the top of the ridge where we could keep everything in sight."

"We need to find Davis," said King.

"Then you go on to the jeep and I'll wait here for Tynan to catch up."

King shook her head and wiped away the sweat. She climbed to her feet and said, "We should both go."

"What about Tynan?"

"He can take care of himself much better than you or I could."

"What is he? One of those Green Berets?"

King laughed and said, "Don't let him hear you call him that. He's in the Navy."

"Oh," said Collins. "Why don't you get going and I'll follow you."

"I'm going to work my way back, deeper into the arroyo before I try to climb up to the ridgeline. Maybe stay on the back side of it once I get to the top so that those men won't be able to see me."

"I'll wait here for a few moments and then come after you," he said.

"Good," she said. For an instant she stood there, wanting to say something more, but not sure what it should be. Finally she turned, and staying close to the slopes of the east wall of the arroyo, began walking off. She skipped a step and then began a slow jog.

Holding the lantern high, Jefferies climbed down from the entrance of the cave. There were rough steps cut into the stone, but they were narrow things that were hard to negotiate. The entrance was narrow, barely shoulder width, and he had to stoop to get in.

Four steps down and he was on the floor of the cave. Ten feet in front of him the opening widened until it was twenty feet across, and farther into the cave it was even bigger. Marks on the walls showed that someone had done that a long time ago. Their broken tools and equipment still lay where they had dropped them so long ago.

The ceiling was also higher, first seven or eight feet over his head, but there was a slight downward slope to the floor so that once they reached the main chamber, the ceiling was fifteen feet high and blackened by the soot of the lamps and torches the Spanish had used to light the interior of the cave.

Without a word, Jefferies moved forward until he came to the point where the chamber widened. Then he stopped and waited. Davis came out then, followed by Winters.

"People have searched for this cave for more than three hundred years," said Winters. "Men have died looking for it. Hell, some of them died trying to protect it. Like that man over there."

Davis turned and sucked in air sharply. The body was little more than a dirty skeleton that was falling apart and partially covered in filthy rags. The skull had rolled away from the main body. One of the leg bones was broken and a hand was missing. There was an arrow in the vertebrae of the neck. The chest was protected by armor, the kind worn by the Spanish conquistadors as they had explored the new world.

"Died trying to keep the Apaches away from the gold. No weapons with the body," said Winters. "I was hoping to find one of those old flintlock pistols, or maybe one of their knives or swords but I guess one of the Apaches carried it away a long time ago."

Davis stared at the skeleton, her eyes wide. She didn't speak.

"Let's move," said Jefferies.

He started forward, deeper into the cave, and Davis followed because he had the lantern. She didn't want to be left in the dark.

Slowly the tunnel widened. The floor was dusty stone. There were footprints in the dust, most of them from modern boots worn by the latest owners of the treasure.

"I don't know exactly what happened in here," said Winters, "but I can make a fairly good guess. The monks, with a small guard of conquistadors, found this cave and discovered that it was rich in gold ore. I suspect they found some other mineral rich areas near here and worked to exploit them all, bringing the ore here for smelting."

They continued on, until the cave narrowed. In the light of the lantern, she could see that someone had built part of a wall and a doorway. An adobe wall and a thick, wooden door that might have protected them for a while, if they were being attacked by Indians.

Winters moved forward like the guide on a tour. "I did some reading in the library and learned that the technique used here is fairly common, or rather was. Spanish built this long before the English were forming their colonies on the east coast."

He turned to face her. "The door was two feet thick, made of wood that had to be imported from fifty miles away and worked on iron hinges, only they didn't have any iron. That's the funny thing. They needed metal and the only metal they had was gold and silver." He pointed at the frame of the door. "Nails and hinges are made of silver. Maybe five, six thousand dollars worth of silver."

Jefferies moved through the door and Winters gestured. "Go on in. Take a look at the treasure that you've been searching for."

Davis stepped forward. She had thought about this moment. She had daydreamed about it. Finding the treasure and seeing it for the first time. The image she normally had was the one that had been drilled into her by movies. Chests filled with jewels that sparkled in the light. Chests filled with gold coins and silver coins.

And it would be brightly lighted. A torch or two on the walls for effect, but there would be bright light from everywhere so that she would be able to see all the treasure. The floor would be clean and the air fresh.

It wasn't that way. She stepped through the doorway,

caught a glimpse of the thick door lying on the cave's floor with its thick silver hinges, and then could see nothing, other than dark shapes.

"All the gold that one person, or two or a dozen could possibly need. Enough gold to make us all wealthy beyond our limited dreams. Enough gold to buy us new cars and boats and houses and all the other things that we haven't been able to afford," said Winters.

"Us," said Jefferies, stressing that word, "but not you. You don't get a share of it because we found it first." He stepped through and held the lantern high.

Her first impression was of a throne room. At the far end was a platform with a chair on it. Two pillars stood on either side of it.

"All gold," said Winters. "The flooring on the raised platform, the throne itself and the pillars. All made of gold. I don't know why they'd waste their time doing it, building it, but they did."

To the right was a wall made of brick. It ran the length of the room, nearly forty feet, and climbed to the ceiling, twenty feet above them.

"Gold," said Winters. "Solid gold. Four feet thick." He pointed across the room where there was a similar wall. "Gold and silver, four feet thick. And look down at the floor. Gold brick a foot thick. Christ, they had the gold."

Davis turned and looked to the rear. In the corner was the remains of an oven used in the smelting process. There were tools scattered around it. And two more skeletons. The skull of one wore a helmet of conquistador design but the other was exposed. Part of the skull was caved in, showing that the man had died violently.

She then noticed the other skeletons scattered around the floor. One lay at the foot of the platform. Two lay to one side and another was slumped behind a pillar. A couple were lying together in a darkened corner, looking as if they had sought refuse there when the fight turned against them. A desperate last hope that had done them no good.

"Must have been quite a fight," said Winters. "Apaches attacking them, killing the guards in the front part of the cave. Killing them one by one and forcing the rest of the men to the rear. Into the chamber." Suddenly he wasn't talking to Davis or to Jefferies, but thinking out loud.

"It would have had to be a surprise attack. One man could hold that narrow opening easily. No one could easily overwhelm him. Maybe they sneaked up at night or maybe approached in the guise of friendlies. I don't know how they did it, but they got in and killed the guard. Once they were through there, they'd have no trouble."

He moved and pointed at the door. "No firing ports. Once it was closed, they were trapped on the inside. But they probably thought they were safe inside." He lifted his hands. "It's cool in here, so they wouldn't have trouble with that. But they probably didn't have any food and there is no natural water around here for them to drink. Eventually they would have to open the door."

He turned and pointed. "You would think they'd build a redoubt of gold, but obviously they didn't. Maybe they thought the Apaches were gone or maybe the Apaches forced their way in. There are evidences of that on the door."

For a moment he was quiet. "The Apaches boiled in, whooping and screaming, waving their stone knives and their war clubs. The first few would have been shot, but once the rifles and then the pistols were empty, it would have been a hand to hand fight. Swords against knives. Man against man. Spanish sword and knife against Apache knife and war club. I think the Spanish probably did all right for a while. But the numbers were against them. They perished here, in this room." He waved a hand indicating the skeletons of the dead soldiers.

"Once the fighting was over, the Apaches retreated taking their dead and wounded with them. They sealed the cave, making it part of their legend, their folklore. No one was to come here again because it was evil. I have heard the legend about the evil here. They had eliminated the evil and if they came back, the evil would come back to get them."

"What bullshit," said Jefferies, breaking the quiet, horrifying mood that Winters had created with his story of Apache attack.

Winters turned and looked at him. "No. Not bullshit," he said quietly. "The Apaches believed it. Once they had sealed the cave, they never came back. You can see that the cave has been sealed all those years, until we found it. They were afraid of the spirits that inhabited this place."

Davis was lost in the story and in the sights around her. The remains of the soldiers who had fought to defend their gold, and then fought to defend themselves. Walls of gold and pillars of gold that we're enough to keep them alive. More gold than the two hundred million that people had talked about.

"My theory," said Winters, "is that they brought everything they took from the ground to this point. They were making gold bars for shipment to Spain, but then decided against it. They stockpiled it here, figuring to take it to Spain later but the Apaches stopped them."

He looked at Davis. "I don't think there was a written record of this place. Just the legends that it had existed without proof."

Davis spoke without thinking. "The records exist," she said, her voice filled with awe. She had never believed that she would see the treasure. It was a lark. Something to do. Like playing the slots in Las Vegas.

"Then you were out here searching," said Jefferies sharply.

"No," she said, but knew it was too late. She'd let them know that she had been searching.

Winters shrugged. He didn't care that much. "Tie her hands and feet."

"No. You don't have to do that."

"We do," said Winters. "We can't let you go until we've made arrangements about this gold. Made arrangements to claim it so that you and your friends can't take it away from us."

Jefferies stepped up to her and set his lantern on the floor. He grabbed her and spun her so she was facing away from him. He jerked her hands behind her.

She looked over her shoulder at him and then back at Winters. "You don't have to tie me up. I'll stay here until you tell me I can leave. I promise."

"Sorry, but I think we do have to tie you up. It's either that or we can kill you right now. Which do you prefer? You make the choice."

She lowered her eyes but didn't answer the question. She felt the rough cord around her wrists. Felt it pulled tight, biting into her tender flesh. She wanted to cry out but didn't make a sound.

"Put her on the platform and tie her ankles," said Winters. "Then we'll go find her friends."

Jefferies led her to the raised platform. She sat down on the edge like someone wanting to dangle her feet in the water off a dock. Jefferies knelt in front of her and ran his hand up the inside of her pant leg until he felt the soft, smooth skin of her calf. He grinned up at her and then removed his hand. Using a short cord, he wrapped it around her ankles a couple of times and then cinched it tight. He stood up and looked at her but didn't touch her again.

Winters picked up the lantern and said, "If you try to get away, I can't be held responsible for the consequences. Stay put and once we've gotten the legalities of the find taken care of, we'll let you go."

Davis sat there quietly for a moment. She pulled at her bonds but there seemed to be no slack in them. "They're too tight," she said. "My hands are getting cold."

"You'll just have to live with it," said Winters. "It'll only be for a couple of hours."

"Don't take the light."

"Sorry. You stay put, you'll be okay. Nothing lives in here. Nothing will get at you. You'll be safe as long as you don't try to do anything stupid."

Winters walked out the door first, followed by Jefferies. As they crossed the wide chamber, Jefferies whispered, "Why keep her alive at all?"

"Because she has friends out here and we might need her as bait. We can always kill her later."

"And what was the crap about staking a claim to the treasure?"

"It was to keep her quiet for now. She may figure out that there is no way for us or anyone else to claim it, but for right now, she thinks we'll be a couple of hours in town and then we'll let her go. As long as she believes that, it'll be easier to handle her."

"So now what?"

"We walk up on her friends, find out who knows they're out here and then get rid of them."

"We should have killed her when we first found her," said Jefferies.

Winters shook his head. "Your trigger happy nature is going to get us into trouble yet."

Jefferies shrugged but didn't say a word.

14

Tynan waited until he was sure that Collins and King were clear of the area. For a moment he considered going after the people who had shot them. He knew they would be amateurs who probably knew nothing about military tactics. Their theory would be to shoot at anything that moved. They wouldn't consider the advantages of the terrain, stealth, or surprise. If they had known anything, they would never have fired until they could have been sure of eliminating the entire threat.

He scanned the ground in front of him. There were shadows dancing and small slides of sand. From the smallest of clues, he knew exactly where his enemies were hiding. They didn't have the sense to sit still. They were shifting around. At least they had given up yelling to each other. He suspected they wanted him to believe they had run away when confronted by other men who were also armed.

The simplist thing to do would be to follow the others back up the arroyo, but he didn't like that. The men here had to know the terrain better than he or those with him did. They were on their home ground. They had selected the battle site.

But they didn't seem to be paying any attention to Tynan. They had fired their shots, yelled a few things and then fallen silent. No more demands about coming out and they wouldn't be hurt. The return fire seemed to have surprised them. Now they were waiting.

Tynan decided that he wasn't going to wait. Carefully, he began to slide to the rear. He kept his eyes focused on the arroyo, looking for signs that the enemy had decided to advance. He crawled backward until he reached a fold in the land on the side of the arroyo, an area where water from the periodic flash floods had eroded a channel two feet deep and three feet wide. It went all the way to the top of the slope.

Tynan flooded into it and crawled up, sticking close to the bottom of it. He climbed up to the top of the ridge and then slipped over the top. Now he was prone, looking down into the arroyo and invisible from the bottom of it. He had expected to see the enemy running along the floor of it, but they still hadn't moved.

Rather than retreat to link with Collins and King, Tynan went the other way. He crept along, his face near the sand, listening for the riflemen. He slipped forward quickly, protected by the lay of the land. When he estimated he had passed the position of the enemy, he crawled to the edge again.

Now he was looking back in the direction from which he had come. He could see three men, two on one side, hiding behind a huge boulder. One of them had a rifle and one a pistol. Closer to him, on the same side of the arroyo as he was, he could see a third man who also had a rifle. None of them were watching the arroyo. They seemed to have given up on everything, but keeping out of the line of fire.

For a moment Tynan considered taking them. The first shot at the man opposite him with the rifle, the second to take the closest rifleman and then turn to deal with the last man who held a pistol. In combat, that's what he'd have done. In Vietnam, that's what he would have done.

But this was Arizona and since there was no clear and present danger, he couldn't haphazardly blaze away at those men, even though they had fired first. They weren't shooting at him and he had the opportunity to run away. The law was a funny thing and Tynan had a life sized picture of himself standing trial for murder because he didn't run when he had the chance.

The best thing to do was slide down the other side of the hill and trot up the valley there until he reached the main ridge and could work his way back to the jeep. Then they could drive into town and tell the sheriff that someone was shooting at the tourists. It was the only legal option available to him.

The shout behind her, stopped her. King turned slowly and saw two men, both armed, staring up at her. Collins stood on the floor of the arroyo, his weapon on the ground and his hands in the air.

"You come on down here, little lady," said one of the men. "Come down slow and easy and no one gets hurt."

King did as she was told, moving carefully until she stood no more than twenty feet away. She tried not to look beyond the men, not wanting to tell them that Tynan was hiding somewhere out there behind them.

"Now, how many of you are there?"

King looked at Collins and then said, "Two."

"Wrong," said the man. "We've already caught one of you."

"Is she all right?" asked Collins. "You've no right to hold us."

"Your lady friend is all right," said the man. "But she's not going to be, and neither are you, until you answer our questions truthfully. Now, how many are there?"

"Three," said King.

"Nope," said the man. "I see two women and one man. Doesn't balance. It's not natural. Four I'd buy. Six I'd buy, but not three."

"That's all there are," said King.

The leader nodded to his companion. He stepped up to Collins and grinned at him. When his eyes locked with Collins's, he swung the butt of his rifle around, smashing the flat of it against the side of Collins's head with a dull thunk. Collins fell to his side, his hands on his temple.

"How many are there?" asked the first man.

"Three," said King.

The leader nodded again.

The man moved toward Collins and kicked him in the stomach. As Collins struggled for breath, the man kicked him in the side and then in the head. Collins jerked once and then collapsed to the sand, not moving. Blood from a cut on his face dripped, staining the sand.

"Once again," said the man. "How many of you are there? And don't try to shit me on this."

King lowered her eyes. She glanced at Collins and then looked away from him. "You want the truth and I give you the truth. Sheila, the woman you hold, is my sister."

The man laughed. "You don't look like sisters."

"We had different fathers. My parents divorced and then Sheila was born when my mother remarried."

The man stood there staring at her. "I don't believe it."

King shrugged. "Nothing I can do to convince you."

The man snapped his fingers. "Get him up, on his feet."

Jefferies reached down and grabbed one of Collins's hands. He tugged on it until Collins was sitting up. His head hung down and he shook it slowly from side to side, trying to clear the cobwebs from it. He climbed to his feet.

"Let's go," said the leader.

"Where?"

"You're in no position to ask," he said. Then he pointed down the arroyo. "Let's just walk down there so that we can join up with the rest of my men." He reached out and grabbed King by the shoulder, shoving her forward.

They began to walk back the way they came. Collins wasn't thinking well because he was hurt. He stumbled once and nearly fell. The men stayed far enough away so that they couldn't be surprised.

King tried to keep from looking at the side of the arroyo where she knew Tynan hid. She was afraid that his attention would be drawn forward and he wouldn't see them coming up behind him until it was too late. And then they turned the corner and Tynan was gone. He had abandoned his position and had not returned the way they had come.

They reached a point where they could almost see to the end of the arroyo. Their captors stopped them and the leader moved forward while Jefferies stayed back to guard the prisoners.

"Hey! Mathews! Jackson! Richards! You people still hiding out there?"

For a few seconds, there was no response. Then one of the men appeared. He studied those in the arroyo for a moment and then yelled, "Hey, Winters. What the hell you doing here?"

"I thought I told you to watch for people running around this area."

Mathews came forward, holding his pistol in one hand. He glanced to the rear and then said, "You said they'd be coming from the desert, not from back here. We stopped them and held them here until you got here."

"They were running away when we found them."

Mathews shrugged and said, "But you've got them so what's the problem."

"How many people you see down here?" asked Winters.

Mathews shrugged. He turned to the right. "Hey, Richards. How many people down here?"

Richards left his hiding place. "I don't know. Three or four. I saw them and shot at them."

"But didn't hit any of them."

"No, I didn't hit any of them."

"So what are we going to do now?" asked Mathews.

"Get all your stuff and come with us. We're going to head back now."

Davis sat in the dark, afraid to move. She waited for her eyes to adjust but there was no light coming in from anywhere. She couldn't see anything. It was as if she had been suddenly struck blind.

With her fingers, she tried to explore the rope around her wrists. She twisted and turned, but couldn't find the knots. There was no play in the ropes so that she couldn't slip her hands free.

It was the same with the ropes around her ankles. Too tight to slip her from her feet. She lifted her legs and stretched out on her stomach. She tried to reach her ankles but failed. She rolled slightly and slid around, getting her legs under her so that she was kneeling. She sat back until her fingers brushed the ropes around her ankles, but she couldn't find the knots there either.

If she could get her feet free, she could have walked to the front of the cave. If she could get her hands free, she could have untied herself. But with her feet tied, the only way she could move would be to hop and she was afraid of falling. There would be no way to stop the fall. She was stuck right where the men had left her.

She stopped struggling and rolled to her side. She lay there resting for a moment and listened. The only sounds were the breath rasping in her throat and the hammering of her own heart. At least they had been right about that. There was nothing in the chamber with her, other than the ghosts of the men killed three hundred years earlier.

From his vantage point at the top of the ridge, looking down into the arroyo, Tynan saw everything that happened. He heard the discussion and then saw the men turn, taking Collins and King with them. Five men, armed with a variety of weapons. The problem was that they had King with them as their prisoner. That changed the situation. There was a kidnapping in progress and he now feared for her life. The rules of engagement had changed. The legal ramifications had changed.

As the people began walking back to the north, Tynan followed them. He stayed on top of the ridge, popping up periodically to check their progress. They walked straight back, never looking for anyone else.

He stopped once and rested. He listened for several minutes, but there didn't seem to be anyone else walking around. He smiled to himself, thinking that he was lucky to get out of there before the men walked up behind him. He'd been getting antsy down there and now he knew why. Somehow he knew that he was in a vulnerable position.

Sometimes he wondered if it was ESP, but figured it was more a subconscious level of observation. The men didn't seem interested in coming to get them and that was because they knew that help was coming shortly from farther up the arroyo. By moving, Tynan had kept them from getting the drop on him.

Now, all he had to do was keep them in sight and wait for the opportunity to free King and the others.

Winters led them to the entrance of the cave. They had left it open, knowing they were going to need to get into it again right away. He pointed and said, "Down there."

"What's inside?" asked King. But she already knew. The descriptions that she'd read told her that these men had found the lost treasure of the Spanish conquistadors and now they were taking steps to protect their find.

"You just go on down inside," said Winters. "You'll see soon enough what's inside."

King didn't move. Jefferies stepped forward and pushed Collins. "Come on, tough guy. Go on down. Nothing in there to hurt you."

"If you don't," said Winters, "we'll be forced to kill you right out here."

"And if we go inside," said King, raising her voice slightly, "you'll kill us anyway."

"We just have to hold you here until we establish a clear claim to our find. Then we'll let you go."

"Bullshit," said Collins.

"Up to you," said Jefferies. "Inside or die out here."

"Go ahead," said King. "There's nothing else we can do about it now."

Collins stepped forward, to the entrance of the cave and peered down, into the gloom. "I can't see anything."

Jefferies handed him the lantern after he had lit it. "Now you can see just fine."

Collins took the lantern and entered the cave. He slipped on the first step because it was so narrow. He caught himself and stood there, holding the lantern out in front of him as he studied the interior.

"You wait out here," said Winters to Mathews.

"Why? I want to see what's on the inside."

"You will soon enough. Just stand out here and make sure that we weren't followed."

"I told you there were only three guys and you've got them all."

"Just do as you're told. You do it right and I'll see that you get a thousand dollar bonus." Winters held up a hand to stop Mathews from speaking. "But you only get the bonus if you don't ask a bunch of stupid questions."

"What about me?" asked Jackson.

"A thousand dollar bonus for each of you, as long as I don't have to spend the next thirty minutes answering a lot of fool questions."

All three of the men shut up then.

"Get moving," Winters ordered Collins.

He stepped down, into the cave proper. King followed him. They walked along the narrow tunnel, followed by their captors until they came to the wide chamber.

"Hold it right there," said Winters.

From deep in the cave came a shout. "That you, Jason?"

"I'm here," he called in response.

Winters grinned and said, "See, we haven't hurt your friend. Just kept her out of the way so that she wouldn't get lost out here. Protected her so she wouldn't get hurt. Kept her here."

"I want to see her," said Collins.

"Oh, you will. And you'll answer a few questions for us. Just a few. Now, through that door."

Collins moved. He still held the light in front of him. As he stepped through, he stopped again and turned right and left. "Oh my God," he said.

King pushed in after him but didn't have to ask what he was looking at. She could see the walls of gold and silver. More than she had expected there to be. Enough to make every one of them in the cave rich, if the men had been willing to share the treasure with anyone else.

"Jason!" yelled Davis.

He turned and saw her lying on the platform, in front of the solid gold chair, still bound. He started toward her. "I'm here, Sheila."

Winters appeared then and ordered him to stop. Then he said, "Questions first and then the family reunion."

"What's he talking about?" asked Davis.

"Your sister is here, with me," said Collins.

"Nice try," said Winters. "Now shut up and let me do the talking."

Davis sat up to wait.

15

The man made it easy on Tynan. He stood with his back to
him, staring down into the cave as if there was something
fascinating below him. Tynan lay above the man, looking
down on him, waiting to see what would happen, waiting
for the men to return, or waiting for someone to start
shooting inside the hidden cave.

Finally he decided that none of those things was going
to happen. Using the cover that was available, he crawled
down off the ridge, keeping his eyes on the man at the
entrance of the cave, waiting for him to turn. But the man
didn't turn. He stood facing away from Tynan like he was
rooted to the ground, his head welded in place.

When Tynan reached the floor of the arroyo, he
stopped. Slowly he came up to his feet and then crouched
there for an instant. Moving slowly, he stood and then
started across the sandy arroyo floor, staying up, on the
balls of his feet, ready to launch himself at the enemy.

But the man kept his face in the cave entrance. When
Tynan was only a few feet away, he leaped at the man. He
landed right behind without a sound. His hands shot out,
grabbed the man under the chin and on the back of the

head. With a single, quick jerk to the left, he snapped the man's neck. There was a quiet popping of bone, a short gasp of pain, and the man slumped, held upright by Tynan.

Moving away from the entrance, Tynan rolled the body out of the way. He left the dead man stretched out on the ground, behind a boulder where he couldn't be seen easily from the cave's mouth.

He moved back then, to the entrance. He looked down and could see the faint light from the lantern at the far end. He took out his pistol, and thumbed back the hammer. Slowly he stepped into the cave, down the steps to the floor. Then he crouched in the shadows, staring into the distance, listening to the quiet buzz of conversation at the far end.

Sticking close to the wall, Tynan slipped out of the narrow passage. He kept his eyes moving, searching the floor under his feet and the walls near him. He came to the bones of the dead Spanish soldier and stepped over him. He stopped then, crouched, and turned. He studied the dirty metal of the chest protector the man had worn. Soldiers should not be left where they fell for scavengers to get at. Soldiers deserved a decent burial. He'd try to take care of that once this was over.

Turning again, he stood, his back to the wall. Across the open floor of the chamber, he could see the glow of white light from the lantern filtering through the door. Standing near it was another of the enemy. Another of the men who had shot at him earlier and who had kidnapped King and Collins.

For a moment he stared at the man and then pulled his eyes away from him. He was afraid that ESP would tell the man that someone else was in the chamber. Better to glance at him than to stare at him.

Tynan moved then, staying in the darkest of the shadows, trying not to hear the conversation. He was afraid that he would hear something that would make him hurry and that was the last thing he needed. Slow and steady, with each move thought out.

He reached the wall of adobe brick. He crouched in the corner and took a deep breath. Snagging the second man would be tougher than grabbing the first. Here there were others close at hand. A wrong move, and those in the other chamber would be alert. They could shoot their prisoners quickly. Stealth was the secret to making it all work.

King knew immediately what would happen. As soon as the men determined that there was no one else out there, they would be shoot the prisoners. Men had killed for a lot less than the gold stored in the one chamber where they stood. Men had killed for the price of a pack of cigarettes. Men had killed for pocket change.

"Son of a bitch," said Jackson, standing in the chamber. He turned in a small circle trying to see everything around him. "Son of a bitch." His voice was filled with awe.

"There's enough here for everyone," said King.

"There's enough here for me and my boys," said Winters. "We found it."

"But there is so much," she said.

"Doesn't matter."

"Listen," said King, "you were right in one respect. We were out here searching, but not for the gold . . ."

"No, you were looking for the lost cities of El Diablo."

"After a fashion," said King, talking fast. "I'm with a university. I'm an archaeologist and we learned that there had been a Spanish settlement around here. Documents uncovered in Seville and Mexico City talked about it. We were interested in finding traces of the settlement." She gestured. "We had no idea that there would be gold."

Winters shook his head. "You take me for an idiot? The woman told us you were looking for the gold."

King nodded. "They were. They thought there was gold out here." She shrugged. "I guess they were right. But the real reason I was here was for the old Spanish settlement."

"Sure."

"Look, there is so much gold that you could buy us off. A million a piece and everyone's happy. Let me have the artifacts." She pointed at the smelter and the tools scattered around it. At the skeletons and the armor. "Let me have that for the university and everyone's happy. No need to kill us."

"All right," said Winters, "for the sake of argument, let's say I agree to your plan. What's to prevent you from running off at the mouth and the next thing I know some government asshole is here claiming the gold for the government?"

"Because we'd lose our share too. Our million, which is a drop in the bucket here."

"Let's just kill them now, Nate," said Jefferies. "No one's going to miss them."

"Not true," said King, holding up her hand. "I'm the advance scout for the university. My job was to survey the area, find out what special equipment we'd need and report back. I don't do that and they're going to know I'm missing. They're going to know where I'm missing."

"Nate, we'll be long gone before they can do anything. Besides, they were looking in the wrong direction."

"Shut up," snapped Winters. "Shut up and let me think."

Collins spoke up then. "I'm an officer stationed at the fort." He pointed at Davis. "Both of us are stationed there.

We don't show up for work tomorrow, and a search is going to be started for us."

"They won't know where to look," said Jefferies.

"They'll find our jeep and start there."

"We can move the jeep. Put it close to the border and let the Mexicans steal it."

"Shut up," said Winters.

"Why are you talking to these people? Let's just kill them now and get it over with."

"We don't kill them," said Winters patiently, "because there are other solutions that are better. You can't kill everyone who walks around in the desert."

"Shit," said Jefferies.

Winters turned toward King. "Your study of the Spanish intrigues me. Did you actually learn about a settlement through Spanish records?"

"Of course. The Spanish kept very good records. The manifests for ships lost between the new world and the old are available. There are a number of treasure ships that were lost in storms off the Florida Keys. The approximate locations of them are known, along with everything they carried."

"She's stalling," said Jefferies.

"Shut up, Lloyd," said Winters.

"We don't have all day," said Jefferies.

"We have as long as I say."

"There is no need for this," said King. "There is so much here that you can buy us off. Why commit a murder, three murders, when you don't have to?"

"It's too late for that argument," snapped Jefferies. "Way to late."

In that moment King knew for sure that Jefferies had been responsible for the murders of the two people that Collins and Davis had found in the desert. She knew the bodies had been moved to protect the entrance to the cave. She knew it as surely as if he had told her about it. He'd even told her how he'd gotten rid of the vehicle so the police would have nothing to go on.

Winters seemed to be the calmer of the two and the leader, but he might not agree to buying them out and that would mean they would all die. She only hoped that Tynan would get there before it was too late. She hoped he would get there before time ran out.

Tynan couldn't hear what was being said on the other side of the adobe wall. It seemed peaceful enough, but he couldn't take the chance. If the gold was in the cave, there was more than enough reason for the men to kill his friends.

He moved slowly, his back to the adobe wall, but now he kept his eyes on the man at the doorway. He put the pistol away because it would be useless to him. If he had to use it, the others would know that he was in the chamber. Firing it would kill his friends as well as the guard.

When he was within striking distance, he crouched, looking up at the man, figuring the angles. As the man straightened up, Tynan struck. His left hand snaked out, snagged the man and jerked him to the rear, his hand covering the man's mouth. As he began to twist and to fall, Tynan slammed his knees into the man's spine, dragging him back.

The man reached up and grabbed Tynan's elbow, trying to jerk the arm free. His fingernails gouged Tynan's flesh. He kicked out, trying to escape but Tynan held tightly. With his right hand on the side of the man's head, Tynan twisted sharply. There was a quiet snap. Tynan felt the man's last breath against the palm of his hand. He went limp suddenly, unmoving. His bowels released as he died.

Quietly, Tynan rolled the man to the floor of the chamber. Then, drawing his pistol, he moved toward the open door. Now he could hear the words. Hear the discussion about the gold and archaeology and sharing the money with each other.

He hesitated there, listening to the voices, trying to place each of the people in the other chamber. King seemed to be to the right, near one of the men. Collins spoke once, from the far side of the chamber, and another of the men seemed to be to the left side of the door. That meant he didn't know where Davis or the third man was.

He'd have felt better if he'd had a flash grenade, but hadn't foreseen the need for one. He would have liked a man or two for back up, but that couldn't be helped. He would have preferred a shotgun to his pistol. All he could do was try to take three men quickly and hope that none of his friends were injured in the firing.

For an instant he closed his eyes and tried to picture the scene on the other side of the door. King standing near one of the men. That would be the first target. Drop that man. Then spin toward the left to hit the second. Concentrate on him, making sure he was down before trying to isolate the last of them.

The odds weren't good. Too many of them to take down too quickly. They'd get some shots off. Directed at him, the others would be safe, but if the men just started shooting, there would be others hurt.

Tynan took a deep breath and leaped through the door, yelling, "Hit the dirt. Hit the dirt."

In the harsh light of the lantern, he saw a man standing, facing King, and he fired once. As the man began to fall, Tynan whirled and fired again. That men shot back, the round snapping past his head. Tynan pulled the trigger a third time. The sound reverberated inside the chamber.

Someone screamed and there was a wet slap of the round striking flesh.

"KILL HIM!" screamed a voice.

"I'm hit. I'm hit."

"Kill him."

Tynan dived for the floor and rolled to his left. He kicked out, knocking King from her feet. He then twisted around and fired at the lantern but missed it.

A shadow ran for the door. Tynan snapped a shot at it. Two. They whined off, into the darkness.

"Help me."

Tynan came up on his knees and fired again, three times, but the man was through the door running. Tynan dived forward and saw the shadow fleeing across the chamber. He fired again and again, the muzzle flash strobing, lighting the interior of the chamber like a camera's flashbulb.

The man took a round in the back and pitched forward. He rolled over and fired back, once, at Tynan. The bullet smashed into the adobe. Dirt exploded from the ancient bricks, cascading down in a choking cloud.

Tynan fired again and the man stopped shooting. Suddenly it was as quiet as a grave in the cave. Nothing moved. Nothing made a sound.

Tynan rolled to the right, out of the doorway and stood up slowly. He turned and saw the bodies sprawled on the floor. King was lying on her stomach, her arms protecting her head. The man near her was lying on his side, groaning quietly. The other was flat on his back, his hand thrown out. Collins was lying near the platform and Davis was on it.

"Everyone okay?" he asked.

King slowly got to her feet and brushed the dirt from her clothes. "I'm fine."

"Sheila?"

"Here. Untie me."

"Jason?"

Nothing.

Tynan walked across the floor and looked down at Collins. There was a ragged stain on his shirt. His face was pale and his breathing was labored.

Tynan looked over his shoulder. "Stevie, grab the weapons. Get them all and then get over to help me."

"What is it?" asked Davis.

"Jason's been hit."

"Is he dead?"

Tynan glanced up at her. "No. He's hurt but not dead."

King dropped the weapons next to him then. "What do you want me to do?"

"Get the lantern over here and then untie Sheila. When you're done, check on the man in the other chamber. I don't want him getting out."

"Why not? Just let him run away."

Tynan glanced at her. "One well placed stick of dynamite, one man with a shovel and half an hour and he could bury this place so that we couldn't get out in a year."

King nodded and stepped up on the platform. She crouched over Davis and struggled with the knots in the rope.

Tynan pulled open Collins's shirt, fearing the worst. He saw the wound, high on the right side, well away from the lungs and the heart. Gently, Tynan rolled the injured man to his back and bent close to look at the wound. He reached under the body and found the exit hole. Through and through.

Using the single large bandage from his first aid kit, he sealed the entry wound. That done, he said, "Give me your first aid kit."

"How is he?" asked King.

"He'll be fine, I think. He'll lose some of the use of his right arm, but he should be okay."

King dropped back to the floor. She looked down at Collins and then at Tynan.

"Take one of the weapons and go look at the man in the chamber. Make sure he's still there. And check that wounded man. I don't want him jumping up."

Reluctantly she picked up one of the pistols and started toward the door. She stopped long enough to determine that Winters was dead. He'd bled to death quickly.

As she moved toward the door, there was an ominous rumble deep in the earth. A quiet but ominous sound and dirt fell from the ceiling.

"We've got to get out of here," said Davis.

"Relax," said Tynan. "This cave has been here for hundreds, thousands of years. It's not going to fall on us."

Davis slipped down beside him and asked, "Anything I can do?"

"Help me bandage his back. Then I think one of us had better go get the jeep and drive it as close to the cave as possible. We need to get him to the hospital. On base."

King was back. "There's one man by the door."

"Should be another about halfway down the chamber."

"Nope," said King. "No one there."

"Shit. Okay. We've got to take a chance and move Jason now. I don't want to get trapped down here. Sheila, I want you to take the legs. Stevie, you and I will pick him up carefully. I want to get both hands under his shoulder so that we don't jerk the wound. You'll need to hold his head and support some of his weight. Everyone understand?"

"Yes," said King.

Tynan got to his knees and carefully worked his hands

under Collins's body. He watched as King knelt on the other side and Davis crouched at his feet.

"Ready?"

Both Davis and King nodded.

"Together now. On three. One. Two. Three."

Slowly they lifted. Collins groaned once. They climbed to their feet.

"Now, slowly, we walk to the door. When we get to the narrow passage, we'll set him down. Then I'll go see what is happening outside."

They worked their way back, out the door and across the wide chamber. When they came to the narrow opening, they slowly set Collins on the ground.

Tynan crouched next to him and took the keys for the jeep from his pocket. He pulled out his pistol then. "I'll go up and make sure that the coast is clear and then get the jeep. Shouldn't be more than thirty minutes."

As he stood up, King grabbed his arm. "What about the treasure?"

"I don't know. We'll think of something later. Right now we've got to get out of here."

King turned and looked back, in the direction from which they'd come. "See? I told you there was gold here. More gold than we thought possible."

"That you did," he said, agreeing.

She stared up at him for an instant. "Good luck, Mark," she said.

"Thanks. I'll be back as quickly as I can." With that he started down the narrow tunnel and the ground under him rumbled as if they'd awakened an angry god who was going to snatch the gold away from them.

16

As Tynan approached the entrance to the cave, he noticed the trail of blood. Not drips, but a trail that led up and out of the cave. The man was badly hurt and Tynan expected to see the body lying on the ground outside the cave.

He blinked in the bright sunlight and hesitated, just inside the entrance. The trail of blood led off, to the left, toward a huge boulder that was sitting on the floor of the arroyo. Tynan peeked out, saw nothing and ducked back.

He hesitated there and then leaped up the last of the steps and out into the afternoon sunshine. As he dived to the right, away from the boulder and the blood trail, there was a shot. Tynan didn't wait to see where it came from. He sprinted across the arroyo floor and dived for cover there. He scrambled up behind several large rocks.

There was a second shot, but it didn't come close. Tynan popped up and looked. Sitting on the ground, his back to the boulder, was the last of the men. He held a gun in his right hand and tried to lift it, but the effort was too much. His shirt was soaked in blood and his head was hanging down, as if he'd gone to sleep.

Tynan lifted his hand, leaned forward against the stones

for support and aimed at the wounded man. But then he
didn't shoot. The man was no longer a threat to him. He
didn't even know that Tynan had gotten out of the cave.
He still watched the entrance. Then, for no reason, he tried
to aim and fire again. The bullet struck the ground thirty
feet in front of him.

That was the last time the man fired. He slumped over
then and was still. Tynan got to his feet and walked slowly
toward the fallen man. It was obvious that he had finally
bled to death there.

Tynan reached the body and took the pistol from the
cold, nerveless fingers. He felt for a pulse and found none.
Satisfied that the last of the men was dead, Tynan turned
and jogged off. He scrambled up the side of the arroyo,
reached the ridgeline and ran along it, toward where they'd
left the jeep parked.

The heat of the afternoon sapped his strength quickly.
His body heated and the sweat poured from him. A head-
ache developed and he was thinking of walking for a
while, but then he saw the jeep and a car sitting in the
distance.

He ran up to them. Quickly, he examined the car, figuring it belonged to one of the men at the cave. There was
nothing he could do about it now.

He walked to the jeep and climbed into the driver's seat.
He used the key to start it and then pulled out. He turned
around, drove down, out of the hills and then turned to the
west, driving over the desert. He found the entrance to the
arroyo and turned up it, hurrying toward the entrance to the
cave.

He stopped at the mouth of the cave and leaped from the
jeep. He hurried back into the cave and found Davis and
King crouched near Collins.

"How's he doing?"

"Restless. Was almost conscious at one point," said King. "He's out of it again. What was that shooting?"

"The man got out but I don't think he had a clue about what was happening. Bled to death before I could get to him."

"How are we going to do this?" asked King.

"I'll take his head and you take his feet. I'll back up and out, you following. Sheila, you go out now and get in the jeep. You take him to the hospital. Once you're there, you call the police and send them out here."

"They'll find the gold."

"Look," said Tynan ignoring the comment. "We're going to have to have a story. Collins is shot and if we don't, the police are going to be all over us. You take him to the hospital and tell them we were jumped by bad guys. There was an exchange of gunfire and Collins was hit. You don't know much about it because you'd gotten separated from us. You don't know what happened. You just send them out here."

"But the gold," she said.

"We'll hide the entrance to the cave. Once this blows over, then we'll all get together to figure out what to do about it," said Tynan. "Now go. And remember that the less you say, the better off you're going to be. You don't know much because you got separated."

"Okay."

"And hurry," said Tynan. "Jason needs to see a doctor quickly."

Davis jammed the jeep into gear and spun the tires as she rocketed back down the arroyo. As she disappeared, King asked, "What are we going to do now?"

"Arrange the scene so that the police will be happy with the scenario. Self defense all the way. And we'll roll some of those rocks in front of the cave's entrance. With luck, the police will buy our story and not look around too hard."

"Gold belongs to the university."

"You try to get it out now and there are going to be legal battles for the next twenty years. Not to mention the fact that our self defense story goes up in smoke. With that much gold around, it's going to look as if we fought over who got what. A falling out among thieves. We'll all end up in jail and someone else will get the gold."

King thought about that for a moment and then nodded. "Everyone and his brother will be down here with a claim to the treasure."

"And the only ones to make any money on it will be the lawyers. They'll get rich with inflated legal fees and we'll end up with nothing other than jail time."

"So what do we do?"

"We've got to bring the bodies out because I found a car and we don't know who it belongs to. And some of the brass from the weapons. We've got to bring it all up and scatter it around. And tell the police that Davis was captured. They were going to kill her if we hadn't gotten here to free her."

"Wouldn't she have said that to them?"

"Right. Well, you were captured. We'll go with that. They were going to kill you if we didn't surrender."

King nodded. "Works good because they told me that they had killed those other two people. Moved the bodies and left their car on the road for the Mexicans to steal."

"They say where the bodies were hidden?"

"Nope. Just that they had moved them."

"Okay," said Tynan, "we'd better get busy."

When the police arrived, Tynan and King were sitting in the shade of the giant boulder. The police approached them carefully, their weapons drawn. Two of them went to check the bodies that were visible. The other two walked toward Tynan and King.

"You armed?"

Tynan surrendered his pistol.

"What happened here?"

Tynan and King told the story they had agreed on. They told it to the officers on the scene and then told it to the sheriff when he arrived and then told it to more officers in an interrogation room with tape recorders running. They gave as much information as they could, moving the final gunfight from the cave to the floor of the arroyo.

They kept it up the rest of the day, stopping long enough to eat some hamburgers and drink a Coke, and then talked into the night. They talked through the night going over the story again and again, telling what King had heard and how Tynan had rescued them.

Finally the sheriff reappeared, dressed in a fresh khaki uniform. He laid a couple of pictures on the table and asked if they had ever seen them before. "They're two missing persons we've got out here."

"Never saw the bodies. Ask Davis."

He laid more pictures on the table and said, "Who are they?"

King identified the man who seemed to be the leader, pointed out the man who had shot the missing people and then shook her head over the other three.

"Hired guns, I guess."

The sheriff slipped into the chair opposite them. He stared at Tynan and then King. "Only thing that bothers me is the motive. Why would these men try to kill you? What do you know that you aren't telling me?"

Tynan shook his head. "We don't understand that either. All we know is that we were out in the desert for a hike and these guys tried to kill us."

"And you took them," said the sheriff.

"I've been trained in such matters," said Tynan. He knew the time had come for the trump card. He pulled one of the note pads toward him, wrote a phone number on it and said, "Call that number, give them my name and ask your questions."

"Area code of two oh two?"

"Washington DC."

The sheriff left and came back five minutes later. "You got some juice," he said. "You're free to go. But I'd like you to hang around for a week or so, while we finish our investigation."

"Well, I'm on leave from the Navy," said Tynan.

"Sightsee," said the sheriff. "People from all over the world come to Arizona to see the sights."

"Good idea," said Tynan.

It took two weeks for them to shake clear of the sheriff and the problems surrounding the lost gold. Davis and Collins agreed to keep quiet about the treasure because it would reopen the case immediately. King would work on finding a way of cashing in on it, with money to be funneled to Collins and Davis as consultants once they had a plan for converting it to cash.

Davis had balked at that. She wanted to return to the cave and pick up a couple of bars to take to Mexico. All three of them talked her out of it. Any of the gold showing up would be a flag to the investigators.

"But we've done nothing wrong," she said.

Tynan pointed out that they had lied to the police and they had covered up evidence. Both of those crimes would be good enough to get them into jail and throw their claims to the treasure into the hopper with all the others.

So they agreed to leave the gold where it was for the

time being, but they would be in touch every six months or so, to decide what the next move would be.

"It's going to be hard," said Davis.

"Of course," agreed King, "but remember, the easiest way for all of us to end up with nothing is for one of us to get greedy. Greed could be the downfall of all of us."

Davis nodded.

John Boyle sat in his favorite bar, in his favorite booth and listened to the country music blaring on the jukebox. The waitress, who was always tired, made a special effort to get his drinks to him because she knew why he was alone. She'd read the story in the paper, along with everyone else. Boyle's friends were dead, suspected of kidnapping, and although the police had talked to him at length, they had let him go.

So now, Boyle sat alone in the booth where he and Winters and Jefferies had spent so much of their time. He drank beers, always ordering three, as if he expected Winters and Jefferies to join him at any moment. But then he'd drink all three of the beers before ordering any more.

And he told stories now. Sometimes, when the bar was quiet and the jukebox turned off, he'd talk of the lost Spanish gold that people knew was hidden somewhere close. Boyle never claimed to know where it was, but he did know it was evil.

"Everyone who touches it dies," he said. "The Spanish stole it from the ground and the Apaches made them put it back. Nate told me that. The Apaches were afraid of it."

Once a man who had stopped by for a beer asked if that was what happened to his friends. Asked if they had found the gold and then died.

"No," said Boyle, his face clouding over. "Searched for

it. We all searched for it, but we never found it. Now they're dead because they looked for it."

"Where?" asked the man.

"Not going to tell," said Boyle. "I do and you'll get out in the desert and die too."

But that was the only time anyone had asked him questions because they knew that he was upset about his friends. They were the only men who had ever befriended him. Boyle had been too snake mean to make friends.

He'd changed with their deaths. He'd become a sad man telling stories and ordering three beers at a time. And no one bothered him.

Back at the university, everyone wanted to know what happened. King told them that she didn't know, except that five men had tried to kill her and Tynan, and that those men had killed two people whose bodies were still missing.

They had a meeting to decide what to do about the treasure. King told them that they couldn't return to look for it now. The opportunity was lost because of the violence near the cave's entrance.

"We were close to it. For a moment we were close," she said, "but we lost the chance."

"It doesn't matter, Doctor King," said the president of the university. "We have a list with another half dozen good prospects on it."

"Such as?"

"There's one that we don't even have to leave the campus to search for. There's one in Virginia. Man named Beale supposedly buried ten or twenty million in gold in one country and then left three coded messages that tell where the treasures can be found. I think that might be the next target."

"How?" asked King.

"We've copies of the codes. Everyone has copies of them. We'll use our computer facilities and see if we can crack the codes and then go dig up the treasure."

King didn't know what to say to him so she kept her mouth shut. She listened as he talked about finding the gold and about the uses for the money. Finally, she got out of there and met Tynan at a small bar for a drink.

"You'll never guess what they're going to do next?"

"Search for the Lost Dutchman."

"Nope, but they're going after another treasure. Didn't learn their lessons from the last fiasco."

"They don't know what happened out there." Tynan lowered his voice. "Besides they were right. We did find the gold."

She took a sip from her drink. "We and everyone else in the county."

"Not everyone, but that's not the point. They went after one specific treasure and they found it. We found it. So maybe it's not such a wild ass scheme after all."

"I don't want to talk about it anymore," she said. "I don't want to think about it either."

"So we need to think about something else. Find a way to occupy our time so that we can't think about it."

"Yeah," agreed King. "We have to find something to do that'll take our minds off the last few weeks."

"Not to mention the fact that I've got to return to duty in a couple of days."

"Not to mention that," said King. "I think I've got an idea that'll help. But we need to get out of here."

"I'm right behind you," said Tynan, standing. "Right behind you."

THE WORLD'S MOST RUTHLESS
FIGHTING UNIT,
TAKING THE ART OF WARFARE
TO THE LIMIT — AND BEYOND!

SEALS #1: AMBUSH!	75189-5/$2.95US/$3.95Can
SEALS #2: BLACKBIRD	75190-9/$2.50US/$3.50Can
SEALS #3: RESCUE!	75191-7/$2.50US/$3.50Can
SEALS #4: TARGET!	75193-3/$2.95US/$3.95Can
SEALS #5: BREAKOUT!	75194-1/$2.95US/$3.95Can
SEALS #6: DESERT RAID	75195-X/$2.95US/$3.95Can
SEALS #7: RECON	75529-7/$2.95US/$3.95Can
SEALS #8: INFILTRATE!	75530-0/$2.95US/$3.95Can
SEALS #9: ASSAULT!	75532-7/$2.95US/$3.95Can
SEALS #10: SNIPER	75533-5/$2.95US/$3.95Can
SEALS #11: ATTACK!	75582-3/$2.95US/$3.95Can
SEALS #12: STRONGHOLD	75583-1/$2.95US/$3.95Can
SEALS #13: CRISIS!	75771-0/$2.95US/$3.50Can

FROM PERSONAL JOURNALS TO BLACKLY HUMOROUS ACCOUNTS

VIETNAM

DISPATCHES, Michael Herr
01976-0/$4.50 US/$5.95 Can

"I believe it may be the best personal journal about war, any war, that any writer has ever accomplished."
—Robert Stone, *Chicago Tribune*

A WORLD OF HURT, Bo Hathaway
69567-7/$3.50 US/$4.50 Can

"War through the eyes of two young soldiers...a painful experience, and an ultimately exhilarating one."
—*Philadelphia Inquirer*

NO BUGLES, NO DRUMS, Charles Durden
69260-0/$3.50 US/$4.50 Can

"The funniest, ghastliest military scenes put to paper since Joseph Heller wrote *Catch-22*"
—*Newsweek*

AMERICAN BOYS, Steven Phillip Smith
67934-5/$4.50 US/$5.95 Can

"The best novel I've come across on the war in Vietnam"
—Norman Mailer

COOKS AND BAKERS, Robert A. Anderson
79590-6/$2.95

"A tough-minded unblinking report from hell"
—*Penthouse*